# Life of A Simple Sailor
# An Autobiography

TO CARRIE

ONE OF THE MOST
WONDERFULLY
DELIGHTFUL
PEOPLE I CAN
EVER KNOW

# Life of A Simple Sailor
# An Autobiography

Joseph C. Powell

American Book Publishers
Newburgh, Indiana

Requests for information should be E-Mailed to
AmericanBookPub@aol.com

ISBN: 0-9720705-8-3

This book is available worldwide via Amazon.com,
BarnesandNoble.com, BooksAMillion.com, or orderable via most
bookstores.

Cover by: Cecilia Brendel
Manuscript Assistant: John Beanblossom

Printed in the United States of America

To my brother Daniel and my sister Kathryn for
making this book possible.

# Life of A Simple Sailor
## An Autobiography

### Prologue

# Prologue

Can you imagine having ten kids? With each new child, how do you find the time to make more? My older siblings fondly tell me the story about how dad would throw pennies in the backyard for them to find. It usually afforded my parents that little time needed for intimacy. And what of the cost? The time and effort it would take to nurture them properly? Compound that with the fact that you're pushing forty when the last one is born. What kind of patience it would take!

Those are probably some of the first questions my father asked himself when he found out his 35-year-old wife was pregnant. Everyone, of course, thought it was wonderful that mom was having one more child. But there was cause for concern, you see. Coupled with the issues above, mother wasn't really in a position to have one more child, as I will explain later. For the next seven months, my mother and this last child were on everyone's mind, except of course mom; only she knew she was having twins.

Sometime after the ninth one was born, mom went through a physical checkup and found that she had finally reached that age when her female "stuff" just wasn't as young as it used to be. The doctor told her that if she had any more children, there would be serious complications. Not only for the child it seemed, but for her as well.

Dad, I'm sure was heartbroken. You see, hopping in the sack was probably one of his greatest hobbies (if you haven't figured that one out on your own) but mom is a devout Catholic, so birth control was out of the question. I've never talked to my father about this but I'm sure he was thinking along these lines...

The options available at this point, assuming mom won't go on the pill, are:

1. Abstinence - Not an option.
2. Mom gets fixed - Doctor recommended no.
3. Dad gets fixed - When hell freezes over.

The easiest way out for dad was for mom to go on the pill. Unfortunately, her (our) religion did not include this in their practices. Can exceptions be made? My father was persistent in getting that question answered.

It wasn't too long after that my parents had petitioned their case to the local diocese for mom to use birth control. They granted their request. Life has taught me many things folks. Let me share this one with you and don't forget it. Like a cat at the dinner table, it never hurts to ask. See? Now everyone's happy. Church is satisfied for mom, and dad loses more pennies.

So, mom went on the pill and subsequently thereafter, conceived. The doctor, of course, was EXTREMELY concerned and monitored my mother throughout all three trimesters. Continuously. Everything seemed to be going okay until the second trimester. The doctor said mom was gaining too much weight and put her on a diet. Not without a fight though.

My mother told the doctor that this pregnancy was a little different from all the others. She told him she thought it was twins. The doctor explained to her that, in the ultrasound, they picked up an image of only one child and, of course this pregnancy was different, all pregnancies are different from each other.

Mom knew about differences in pregnancies, she explained this to the doctor adding to the fact that this was her tenth (eleventh?) one. But in the end, with my father's support, the doctor won. Mom went on a diet.

Seven months after conception, she went into labor. It was a Friday afternoon. Early in the morning on Monday, I saw the world for the first time. I was just over 2 pounds. So much for pregnancy diets. Wouldn't you agree?

Pulling his gloves off, the doctor starts wrapping things up when my mother exclaimed that another was on its way. Sternly, the doctor looked at my mom and began the same "Your-Not-Having-Twins" speech when he noticed my twin brother's head popping out. He was just over one pound. (For the record, he is a little uglier too…)

The doctor of course, trying to salvage his dignity, couldn't stop talking about the image of only one child in the ultrasound. But you know what? Shame on him. Throughout the dozens of checkups he performed on my mom during the pregnancy, he never listened to her, or the faint, tiny sound of my twin's second heart beat behind mine.

With God's blessings, we both turned out okay. Well, I was, anyway. And after a month in the incubator, we were ready to join the family. Now, let's fast-forward about 17 years.

My senior year in high school, dad quit his job for his own reasons and purchased a small restaurant. Money was tight now. All my parents' efforts, and money, were pumped into this place. I was looking at colleges, but knew it would really be a burden for my parents to pay for it, so I joined the NAVY.

Hindsight tells me that I could have received aid for part of it and I could take care of the rest myself (believe me, I can do anything), but I was young then and wasn't thinking clearly, I suppose. But joining the NAVY was one of the best moves I ever made. I have experienced so much in life, so much to treasure. Before I reached the age of 30, I have been to over 40 different countries in 4 different continents. Before the age of 30, I have lived a full life of adventure. Some memories are good, some of them not so good, but all were memorable.

So, here it is....

# Chapter 1

My first duty assignment was on a little island in the South Pacific called Guam. Not the end of the world, but you can certainly see it from there. I was miserable when I arrived. No family, no friends, just me on this rock. It was the first time I have ever been away from my family. I really missed them. Before I joined the NAVY, I never really left my block, let alone travel to a foreign country. So there I was, alone.

I must have felt sorry for myself for the first six months. I moped around a bit and did a lot of nothing except work. Being an Engineer in the NAVY, there was certainly plenty of that to go around. It really wasn't difficult to keep myself occupied. During the first few weeks into my assignment, my Chief took me under his wing to train me on the Engineering Plant. I worked down in the Boiler Room and we were in our upkeep period, so the plant was not online.

During this period of upkeep, we were afforded the opportunity to do sorely needed maintenance on some of the equipment that was off-line. My Chief took me down there one day and showed me how to change an O-ring on a lube oil strainer for the Forced Draft Blower; a mechanical device used to force air into the boiler for combustion. Pulling out his tool bag, he grabbed a few items out to include: tools, rags and repair parts for the blower. Then, he sat down on the deck plates and motioned for me to do the same.

My Chief began to explain to me that at this point in the NAVY's career, they were moving forward with phasing out boiler-driven ships, and replacing them with Gas Turbine ships. So all the repair parts that were commonplace in the past, were hard to appropriate now. Specifically speaking, this O-ring. We only had two on board the ship and my Chief wanted me to understand that the Supply Officer had not been successful in obtaining any more for the blower.

Not to change the subject, and while he was teaching me how to change this O-ring, my Chief talked about diving in the ocean and how this place was one of the best spots for it. He told me that every weekend he and some others would go in the water for an hour or two to spear fish, or just to explore. I felt as if he was probing me to see if I would like to come along one day with them, so I showed some interest. Frankly, I never really thought about it before, but I didn't tell him that.

Before I knew it, the replacement of the ring was complete and my mentor changed the subject once again. With one more O-ring left, he held it up in front of me and said, "Powell, this is the last O-ring on the ship for the blowers. We cannot purchase anymore. The NAVY is fazing us out, so all repair parts have been discontinued. The other blower is going to need this O-ring in the months to follow. I want you to hold onto it and never lose it, or it's your butt." Then, he handed it over to me.

So, I took my charge in my hand. For the first time, I have been given responsibility, albeit small. Smiling to myself, I removed my shoe and sock. Then, I took the O-ring and placed it over my foot and around my ankle. Putting my sock and shoe back on, I looked back up at my Chief for approval. He just smiled and said; "Think about the diving, Powell," as he walked away.

That following weekend, my Chief approached me while I was in my rack and asked me to come along for a dive. I wasn't certified at the time but was willing to give it a shot. Weekends were quite the bore anyway. I would just tuck myself away in my rack, read a book or two, and sleep. All my peers were married or, at least, had a significant other and I had absolutely nothing in common with any of them. But it was time for me to just grow up. I decided it was time to sink or swim. Pardon the pun.

So a few hours later on that clear, Saturday morning, we threw on our gear and dove in Apra Harbor.

A marvelous place to dive, the Mariana Islands are possibly one of the best places to go for a pleasant swim. Since then, I dove the Trench, the Great Barrier Reef, Virgin Islands, Mediterranean, to name a few. But nothing compares to the pastel beauty of the Mariana's reefs. The water is so clear; if you looked hard enough, you could see for a mile away.

Our target was a Japanese battle ship resting on top of an old Spanish galleon at the bottom of the harbor. We brought along spear guns for hunting, not protection, but I'm glad I had it with me. I think it saved my life. It was our intention to cook whatever we caught that night. Prior to getting into the water, we had prepared a huge pot on the beach in which everything we caught would go into.

Now, Guam is surrounded by coral reefs. Large sharks can't really get in. Once in a blue moon though, the water level rises high enough to were a formidable one can sneak in. However, along with a large reef system, comes a plentiful food supply. Thankfully, the sharks normally kept to themselves. As a matter of fact, the only story I had heard about a shark attack on Guam was back in the 50s. A young lady was attacked while snorkeling in the water. She really shouldn't have been there at the time. She was on her menstruation cycle, and I guess whatever device she was using to stop the blood flow started to malfunction at the wrong time.

So, as you can see, shark attacks are what you would call rare in Guam. It was just my luck that 35 years later two more shark attacks would happen. Both of them had my name written all over it. I'm such a blessed child.

The second shark encounter isn't much to brag about. I had speared a fish at close range. While holding it in my hand, and out of nowhere, a black tip charged in and grabbed it, along with my hand. He shook me around a bit, but besides the little bragging scar on my hand, I left with only soiled pants.

But the first shark encounter could have been quite devastating. Like I said, I'm glad I had that spear gun.

It just so happens that a week prior to the dive, we had one of those high rises to the water level and it brought with her a 14-foot Hammerhead shark. The islanders called it Charlie and besides a few distant sightings, Charlie pretty much behaved himself. Until, of course, I got into the water.

One of the people with me was a Samoan. He was small for his race, only 6' 6", 300 pounds but pretty tough, nonetheless. He was really an enjoyable fellow but liked making me the blunt end of all his jokes. I think I was his favorite.

I don't know how he spotted it, let alone catch it with his hands, but we were in about 5 feet when he motioned for me to surface with him. He had caught an octopus and wanted to show it to me. So we both surfaced and as I took off my mask, he proudly displayed his prize. There, clutched in his huge fist, I could see this wet, slimy thing wriggling in desperation.

Let's call him Molly. Molly also liked to teach me odd islander things, just to see my reaction I think. Today, he was going to teach me the proper way to eat octopus. Grabbing one of the tentacles, he placed the tip of it in his mouth and slurped it up like a spaghetti noodle. Once he reached the base, he bit it off and swallowed. Smiling at me with his huge, bloody teeth, he handed his prize over to me requesting that I do the same. What an initiation!

I knew he was at his old tricks, but I wasn't about to let him think that this 5' 7", 150-pound man was a wimp. So I grabbed that octopus and did the same. I almost threw up. It wasn't the taste or thought that triggered the sensation; it was the constant wiggle in my stomach. Molly could see the shock in my eyes. He just laughed and patted me on the shoulder. What a good sport I was for him.

We descended about fifty feet, spearing fish on our way down to the wreck sight. Now my Chief was a nut. He would spear anything if it moved. I remember one time a large nurse shark crossed my path rather quickly, trying to escape from something. It wasn't moments later when my Chief bowled me over, chasing that shark with his gun.

This time my Chief, who was about ten feet away, speared a Lappal-Lappal, a small grouper, at close range. Now, his spear gun was the magnum of spear guns. Very powerful, and at such close range, he nearly tore the fish in half. Knowing that the only thing this fish could do now was bleed; he decided to toss it aside. You really don't want something like that at your side in the ocean, if you know what I mean.

Nearing the wreck site, I noticed all these fish scales raining down around me like snowflakes. I looked up and there he was — Charlie, making a meal of this Lappal-Lappal. I looked around quickly for my companions to warn them, but they had moved too far away to notice me now. I've never been taught how to fend off sharks or how to escape. I was really scared. So I did what I thought was right. I swam backwards, facing the shark. All of a sudden, it disappeared.

I reached a cropping of reef and grabbed it. Holding on, I'm looking back and forth, I had lost sight of my partners. I knew the shark could be anywhere. Realizing that, if anything else, my air supply running out will kill me, I steeled myself to leave the security of the reef. I needed to find my friends. And then suddenly, out of nowhere, it attacked.

The first pass cost me my fish bag. Charlie grabbed it and tore it from my dive belt fiercely. It spun me around, placing me in shock. I could clearly see him gulp my fish, bag and all. I could see the bulge move slowly down the length of his body until it rested in his belly. The second pass was for me.

Turning back toward me, he picked up speed. I could see the nictitating membrane cover his eyes, indicating he was ready to strike. And there I was, as vulnerable as a babe. I didn't know what to do. But something else I have learned in life, when you're about ready to die, life does not flash before your eyes. I'm sure it's different for everyone, but for me a calm state resides over me. A feeling I have had the misfortune to experience several times hence.

He struck about chest level, mouth gaping open. You would think that a hammer has a small mouth; proportionally speaking, it does. But this was a 14-footer. His mouth was huge. I could see the tiny air bubbles escaping from the rows of teeth in his jaws, scraps of flesh fluttering between them. That's all I saw as he moved his hammer-like head to the side to get a good bite. I did not hesitate.

I grabbed each side of his head with each of my hands. It was difficult to hold onto. But my gloved fingers dug in deep. Shocked, the shark stopped for a second, and then swam forward, slower this time, moving his head back and forth to unhook me. His mouth was opening and closing at the same slow speed. He was pushing me backward and down. I had no idea what was behind me. That's what I was thinking about. Go figure.

And then he finally came; Molly. He grabbed my spear gun off my side and rammed it into the gills of the shark. It went into momentary convulsions, I lost my grip and it was free. Molly lost hold of my spear gun and it fell slowly to the bottom. I started to swim backwards again, with Molly this time, keeping our eyes on the shark.

Recovering from its wound, superficial as it was, Charlie turned toward me once again. He was more cautious this time. He circled us three times before it decided to strike again. Molly grabbed his spear gun and swiftly cocked it, preparing for battle. I was unarmed. But Molly's performance earlier had armed me with a more powerful weapon, courage and determination. I was only 18, but if I was going to die on the shark's turf, it was going to be on my terms.

I looked over to Molly and saw his diving-knife at his ankle. I grabbed it and then put five feet of distance between Molly and me. The shark came for Molly this time. He let loose his spear gun, trying to catch it in the sharks mouth as it opened. It missed its target barely, grazing the "chin" of the shark. Again, the shark paused. Now was my chance.

Mimicking Molly, I came on the top part of the shark and thrust the knife deep in its gills. With my other hand, I shoved it in the other gill and grabbed tight. I could feel the jaws working. Blood started to flow from both sides of the gills and the shark shook violently. I smiled to myself, of all places. I felt like a cowboy riding a bull. What a thought to have at a time like this.

It didn't take long for the shark to shake me loose. But I'm sure I would have won a golden belt buckle if I were in Texas. Relief washed over me as I saw the shark spiraling downward, still convulsing. Molly grabbed my arm. It was time to leave. We made our ascent upward quickly, but cautiously. It would have been a shame to survive something like this only to die from the binge. I couldn't understand that at the time. I just wanted to get the hell out of there. Another reason to thank Molly.

Once at the surface, we saw the others on the boat. They were shouting their warnings about the shark. Apparently, they thought imminent danger was still afoot. They were throwing out lifelines and rope. One of them had a rifle with him. Customarily carried by sailors to scare off sharks. We quickly boarded.

The Chief told us that they had spotted Charlie, surfaced and jumped into the boat. It wasn't until afterwards that they notice Molly and I were not with them. After calming myself down a bit (it took Molly much longer; he was scared), I told them the story about what happened. They, of course didn't believe me. Then Molly stepped in to bring credibility to my story. They still didn't believe us. But at least they were a bit more respectful this time. After all, truth or not, and how upset he plainly was, you gave respect to a man Molly's size.

But they still didn't believe us. It was pretty spooky. No one encounters a 14-foot hammerhead shark and is in the position to talk about it seconds later. It was just hard for them to swallow. That is, not until Molly grabbed my hand and lifted it up high for everyone to see. I was at a loss for words when I saw that I was holding part of the shark's gill.

That night, lying in my rack aboard my ship, I couldn't sleep. It wasn't the memories of what happened that day, or the thought that I could have died. It was more than likely just in my head but I could still feel that damn wiggling in my stomach.

# Chapter 2

We pulled into Thailand during the Water Festival, a fun holiday. A century or so ago, Thailand went through a serious drought that nearly wiped out their civilization. I don't really know the details or statistics but it nearly devastated them completely. Crops had died, food supply ran low; it was a rough time for them, I could only imagine.

The rains eventually came back and nurtured their civilization back to health. Every year thereafter they celebrated the event, giving birth to the Water Festival. We arrived at the beginning of it.

For this festival, you need something that contains water and is easily dispatched onto another individual, like water guns, balloons, even trash cans if you are that capable. Our weapon of choice was the water gun. Because we were Americans, the local islanders took great pleasure in paying us special attention. You would think that a group of military personnel would be quite capable of holding their own in a gunfight. Needless to say, we lost miserably. It was time to retreat.

Most people would find sanctuary in a church but we're sailors, right? We found our refuge in a local bar called the Casablanca. I was introduced to a wonderful, but dangerous, refreshment called Yeagermiester. Wow, what an impact. After several shots of this stuff, I decided to wage war on the bartender and her waitress. Well, they started it really, but I was in the mood to finish it.

After the bartender and waitress plummeted me with water balloons, my shipmate and I went into the head to get some water. We found a gold mine. Sitting in the center of the restroom was a 55-gallon trashcan already filled with water. We picked it up and carried it out to use on our generous hosts.

Seeing us, the bartender grabbed trash bags to cover up all the electrical stuff she had like her stereo, cash register and the ilk. We paid no attention to her, didn't wish to disturb her work. Rather, we zeroed in on the waitress and dumped it on her. I won't get into what happened in the battle, but the 5 of us sailors defeated our enemy of two women and celebrated our glorious victory with another shot of Yeagermeister and a cigar. The bar at this time was a foot deep in water. I guess we showed them.

No damage was done of course; it was all in good fun. But we compensated our hosts with $100 American. We sat with them and inquired about the wonders of Thailand. The story that really intrigued us was about kickboxing, something Thailand is famous for. As a matter of fact, you can't throw a stone without hitting an establishment that conducts a boxing show. We decided to go to one the next day.

The following day we followed the directions provided by our ladies the previous day and easily found a kickboxing ring. We walked into a smoke-filled, rowdy place that had no seats available for us. We weeded our way as close to the ring as possible. You won't believe what we saw next.

First, let me tell you how this works. Anybody can jump up there to fight. Anybody. The house usually has their favorite, generally employed by the house, and all the competitors (and subsequent revenue) comes from suckers like us. So the house thought anyway. If you wish to fight, you pay a certain dollar amount to the kitty and, if you win, you take home the kitty. Believe me on this (another thing I learned), you will have better odds in Vegas than you will as a tourist at a kickboxing ring in Thailand.

So, we snuggled up to the ring for a show and here is what we saw. In the center of the ring was a young Marine, padded up and wearing a football helmet. He was crouched on the floor of the mat, head between his knees and pouting like a child with an orangutan sitting on top of him pounding away! GOOD LORD, what a sight.

The Marine didn't last one round. We watched several bouts, no one lasted a single round. After the bell rang, all the padded competitors found themselves in the same position as the Marine (except for the crying part), getting knocked to pieces before the bell tolled again to end the round. Apparently, if you survived one round with the orangutan, you win. But like I said, no one lasted one round. But I was watching...

After observing 10 or so rounds, I figured it out. The light bulb above my head was nearly tangible. Snapping my fingers, I walked up to the ref before my shipmates could stop me. Sadly enough, they didn't even want to. They needed a good story to bring back to the ship, I suppose. I looked back at them as I climbed the ring and they were cheering me on and laughing their hearts out. What support.

I gave my money to the ref and he had a team of guys pad me up. I was getting nervous, but I knew I had this beat. The people donning my gear were talking in their foreign tongue; I didn't understand a word of it. I am sure, however, that remarks like "stupid", "sucker" and "loser" were in there. Then it was time. I could do this!

Once the bell rang, and before the ape could move, I removed my helmet and tossed it to the side. At that point, I wasn't so certain it was going to work. The orangutan just stood there for a moment, confusion crossed its face. I couldn't hear my shipmates yelling in concern in the background. The roar of the crowd drowned them out. Just then, the orangutan made its move.

Straight for the helmet it went. Luckily, for once in my life, I was right. The orangutan was trained to beat the helmet at the sound of the bell. I looked over to the ref who had daggers in his eyes. Before he could react though, I went behind the orangutan and executed a "full-nelson," an illegal, Greco-Roman wrestling hold that I always dreamed of using back in my days of wrestling in high school. I know the average ape is far stronger than the average man, so I held tight, VERY tight. Instantaniously, the orangutan's neck broke and was dead.

If I can take this time out right now for all the Green-Peace'ers and tree-huggers, I AM an animal activist. I love animals and it breaks my heart to no end that I killed this magnificent creature. But it happened and the past can't be changed. There you have it. Now, go find yourself a nice tree.

Very upset over losing their orangutan, but true to their word, I won the kitty. Oh, they gave me the orangutan as well. I guess they didn't need it anymore. So here it is, 02:00 going back to the ship with a dead orangutan. Dragging it back by the scruff of its neck. When we crossed the brow, the Quarterdeck watch didn't say much. They've seen worse cross the brow. (Once I crossed the Quarterdeck in a Russian sailor uniform. I'm not certain if I can tell that story yet. I'll have to get back with you on that one.)

We took the ape down to the Engineering Berthing, put a baseball cap on it, sat it in a chair facing the TV and then went to bed. As an afterthought, and right before we stepped out, one of the sailors turned the TV on for our guest. He had more to drink than me.

We woke up to Reveille that morning. I was tired, hung over and COMPLETELY forgot about the orangutan. I carried out my duties in the normal fashion.

I suppose it was the Executive Officer that discovered the ape first and told the Skipper. Or at least was the first one to do something about it. Neither would surprise me.

But once he found out, the Skipper spoke to the crew on the P.A. system. First, he thanked us all for being great Ambassadors for the American people. No one got into any serious trouble (a sailor usually does) while there in Thailand. The Skipper then went over a few things about our upcoming visits to Australia and the Philippines, as well as a few exercises we were tasked to perform while underway.

What the skipper said next, I will never forget. I'll just give it to you almost word for word. "...And by the way, WHOEVER PLACED THAT F#C#ING MONKEY ON MY SHIP HAS 5 MINUTES TO MAKE IT DISAPPEAR OR LIBERTY IS SECURED FOR EVERYONE FOR THE REST OF THIS CRUISE!"

It was at that moment I finally remembered what had happened. I wasn't really certain what to do at this point. But I knew I had to get that orangutan. Fortunately, sailors stick out for each other. They all turned their backs to anyone who had that "Oh-Sh#t" look on their face. The five of us who were the guilty party snuck down in Engineering Berthing, grabbed the orangutan and dumped him over the side. Thankfully, no one said a word.

# Chapter 3

Ok, this one I really don't expect you to believe. God knows, not even my family buys it, but they enjoy the story. Perhaps you will too.

I was brand new to the NAVY world, just 19 years old when we pulled into the Philippines. We moored on a remote peninsula called Navasan Pier, an ammo dump. Ships would pull into this particular pier to load up on all types of ammo; I can't mention what kinds of course.

Just like every time we had pulled into there in the past, we would moor the ship early in the morning and shut down the Engineering Plants. "Cold Iron" status we would call it. Once there and the ship turned off, there really wasn't much for us to do. So, we would idly sit by playing cards, watching movies or writing letters, until that call from heaven came: "Liberty Call, Liberty Call..."

Thing is, we had to muster at 07:00, but couldn't leave the ship until 17:00. This was in fact a great time for rest and relaxation. Sailors at sea are some of the hardest working, long-houred people you will ever meet. It wasn't uncommon to work 18 to 20 hours per day. The most unsettling thing is that you actually got used to it. You may know this "robot-mode" in which I speak of. If you do, I'm sorry.

While there, the Engineers would designate one person to make logistic runs from the ship to the base. Between the two was about 50 miles of jungle. Because the idle time was so precious to the crew, the person designated to do the supply runs was usually the new kid on the block. That was me. So they gave me the keys to my vehicle, gave me my orders and shoved me off. It was the "sh#t job", as they liked to call it. And I was to do this every day for the entire three weeks we were there.

Walking across the pier, I made my way to the small hangar that held my vehicle. I would need to drive it to the ship first in order to pick up several things that needed to go to the base. Then off I would go. I had never been to the Philippines before, but they told me it was a one-road trip to the base. I didn't need directions. The only guidelines they gave me was to stay on the road while in the jungle and don't make any side trips down the paths that said, "RESTRICTED, DO NOT ENTER."

This was easy enough, I thought to myself as I slid open the hangar door. What I saw next just put a grin on my face from ear to ear. It appears as if my vehicle was going to be a Hummer. Let me ask you this: 19 year old kid, 50 miles of jungle in a Hummer, no supervision; is this truly a "sh#t" assignment? As I thought that, my grin widened. I think not.

As I pulled up to the ship, I tried to contain my excitement. I didn't want to lose this opportunity to "test drive" the Hummer. I put on my best "this-is-not-fair" face. It must have worked. They loaded up the

Hummer without making me do any of the work. I sat back and watched them sweat. I was just all too excited to get on the road.

Once loaded, I was off. I drove carefully for the first mile to ensure no one was in eyesight. After that, I floored it. I stayed true to my word and did not enter any restricted areas, but I'm afraid I failed miserably on staying on the road. I must say, short of a ten-foot diameter oak, a Hummer can plow through most anything. I tested it on hills, streams and small boulders. It was a blast. I lost track of time.

I didn't really notice my lapse in duty until I stumbled across the road again. After chastising myself, I faithfully played out my mission. I stayed true to my course, taking the only road that had lead to base. Placing the vehicle at a nice, leisurely speed limit, I comfortably made my approach toward the base.

At a certain part of the jungle, I noticed several family groups of monkeys jumping around. I slowed my pace a bit to get a better look at them. Slowing down afforded these monkeys to take a closer look at me too. They jumped all over the Hummer, swinging on the roll bars, sitting on the hood, enjoying the breeze. It was fascinating. They seemed fascinated as well.

Not much surprises me anymore, I've seen and have done a lot in my life, but what happened next was one of the most unbelievable and shocking things I have ever seen. One of these monkeys came on top of the hood and sat down upon it, facing the opposite direction of me. He seemed to be having a wonderful time. No thought whatsoever about being in my line of vision. I considered that rude, but he was a monkey. I was willing to give him a little latitude.... Until he turned around and faced me, that is.

Facing me through the windshield, he was still in my line of sight. I had to shift my head to the side a little to take him out of it. As I shifted my head to the right, he shifted his body to the left to stay in my line of sight. So, I shifted to the left, and then he shifted to the right. Back and forth we played this game. I could swear he was smiling.

I stopped my Hummer and was going to scold him, as if that would do any good. But right before I could point my finger at him and speak a single syllable, he stood up, jumped on the roll bar above me, twirled a few times, launched himself off and landed right in the passenger seat. He looked at me and smiled again. Whatever. As if I could speak "monkey."

That wasn't the shocking part though. This is: after sizing me up to see if I would shoo him away, he grabbed the seat belt and locked himself into place. I put the stopped Hummer in park now and looked back at him. He looked back up at me, saluted, and indicated that he wanted me to continue on. I can't really say how. He was waving his arms in the air all over the place. I surmised that was monkey talk for "let's go."

Who am I to argue with a monkey? I thought I was crazy enough just letting him become a passenger. So, off we went to base.

Once reaching the base, I strolled to a stop. The monkey unhooked his seat belt, gave me another salute and left the vehicle. He went to go do monkey stuff, I suppose. And me? Well, I had to work. I pulled out my map of the base as I watched my little friend take off. Finding my first target on the map, I started the Hummer again and headed in the right direction.

It took me about four hours to complete my task. I sat in my Hummer and reviewed my checklist again to ensure I accomplished everything. I took the valves to the repair shop that needed overhauling, submitted the supply requisitions to the Supply Department, dropped off some letters to the Post Office for the Postal Clerks and picked up a Snickers bar for my Chief. No, I wasn't sucking up. He liked Snickers bars and the ship had none. He was my direct supervisor and he told me that if I don't accomplish anything else, I better bring back some Snickers bars or he would stick me in the boiler for a day. Who was I to argue with a Chief?

While I was looking at my checklist, my monkey friend came back. He just plopped himself in and fastened his seatbelt as if he owned the place. It appeared he had a checklist to follow as well, albeit smaller. He was carrying a small bushel of bananas. I didn't ask him were he got it. He probably stole it from some poor vendor trying to keep his daughter out of prostitution. Besides, I was beginning to like my little thief. So instead, I rendered a salute to him this time, and then off we went back into the jungle.

Once we reached the certain part of the jungle where we originally met, He unbuckled his seatbelt, gave me another salute, and disappeared into the jungle with bananas in tow. I thought for a minute on how I was going to explain all this to my Chief, and then I figured, it was just too outlandish to describe it, so better just keep my mouth shut. And silence was the best policy, up until the following week, that is. My little thief put me in considerable risk of trouble.

As I mentioned earlier, I had to make these trips every day for three weeks. And as sure as the sun sets, my monkey rendezvoused with me every day at the same spot in the jungle and buckled himself in. Everyday, we went to the base. I would go do my things, he would do his, and we both would meet when it was time to go back to the ship. He would catch a ride until we reached his spot in the jungle and then he would leave.

Like I mentioned also, he would have his own agenda and bring back his little list of items. It always ranged from bananas to pineapples and mangos. He even brought back a pair of girl's underwear, (even monkeys have weaknesses I suppose). But once he brought back a Military I.D. Card. This was something he just should not have had. And it is what put me in a very tight spot.

I took the I.D. away from him thinking I would return it the next day to the base police. He protested a bit, but I was the boss, after all. So I brought it on board with me and put it in my locker.

That evening, our ship had a surprise locker inspection. Apparently, Someone had his money stolen that day. Even though I wasn't there, I had to have mine inspected as well. No partial-ism in the NAVY. Needless to say, they found the I.D. card.

The Master-At-Arms confiscated it and asked me where I got it. I was pretty honest with him except I didn't tell him about the monkey, I told him I found it and was going to turn it in at the base tomorrow. The Master-At-Arms asked me to stay put and then he left.

He returned some 15 minutes later and said that he just called the Master-At-Arms on base and informed me that the I.D. was reported stolen yesterday. He also told me that the I.D. was stolen out of a sailor's wallet at home. The sailor had it on his nightstand by the bed and swears he left it there that morning where it stayed put all day. Until it was stolen of course. How do I explain that?

My Chief strolled up at that time and saw that things just didn't add up, especially when he looked into my eyes. Now I was a good sailor and never really got into any trouble at that point. Later on in my career I will gleefully recant that statement. But at that point, I never put myself in any real mischief. My Chief however knew I was hiding something. So, before the Master-At-Arms could put the proverbial cuffs on me, my Chief asked the favor to handle it on his own terms. The Master-At-Arms conceded, if not for mutual respect, for rank. Chiefs control the NAVY.

My Chief took me to his stateroom and sat me down. I figured things couldn't be any worse so I just told him God's honest truth. He, of course, did not believe me. But he had a great laugh. He told me that in all his years in the NAVY, he had heard just about anything spout out of a sailor's mouth to keep himself out of trouble but never anything as crazy as this.

I was getting a little desperate now. I wasn't certain on how to handle this. There was only one thing I really could do. I challenged my Chief to come along with me on the next logistics run to see for himself. Humoring me, he said ok. I don't know if it was the chance to get away from the ship, to give a sailor the benefit of the doubt, or the conviction in my eyes that made him agree. Or maybe it was the Snickers bar. I don't know, but I was thankful for the chance to prove my innocence.

The next morning after muster and breakfast, we hopped into the Hummer, ready to leave. My Chief got into the passenger's seat. I looked over at him and, looking as sheepishly as I could, asked him to move into the back seat. He was sitting in my monkey's seat. He looked EXTEMELY offended. Wouldn't you? Having to give up your seat for a monkey? But he agreed saying "If that fu#*ing monkey doesn't show up, I'm hauling your butt to the brig myself!"

I gulped down a swallow of air. That would be worse than going in a boiler for a day. I never wished to have a Snickers bar as much as I did at that point. And yes, that would have been considered sucking up.

Going into the jungle, my Chief just began to realize what kind of treat was offered to me. A Hummer and 50 miles of jungle, that is. He mentioned this fact to me. Shoot, I really didn't want anyone to catch on. I was having way too much fun. I didn't want the task taken away from me by a senior sailor. I did know, however, that if my monkey didn't show up, it would. He had better be there.

Sure as his consistency, we reached that part of the jungle and there he was. I slowed down a bit, like I always did, to afford him the opportunity to get in, but he was quite ambivalent due to my Chief in the back seat. I started to sweat. But then he came in, sat down and put on his seat belt. He then looked back at my Chief, sized him up, and rendered a salute to him. Whew!

My Chief pretty much kept to himself the rest of the way to base. I would look back at him from time to time through the rearview mirror. He had the look of disbelief in his eyes. I, on the other hand, had the look of vindication.

After all was said and done, though my Chief didn't spill the beans about my monkey, he did get me out of hot water. I don't know what he said or did, but I never heard about the I.D. card again. Like I said,

Chiefs indeed control the NAVY.

# Chapter 4

I want all of you to do me a favor. If you ever get lost and can't find your way, whether it's in the United States or abroad, I want you to think of this story. Things could get worse for you. Always remember this, you can accomplish anything with a little patience and determination. These are two of the greatest assets to have when accomplishing goals. I had the opportunity to exercise those skills upon transferring to another duty station. I hope you never have it as rough as this.

I spent my last evening onboard this particular ship, excited to no end. I couldn't sleep. Tomorrow, I would catch a ride to the airport and go back to the United States. There's no place like home. Everything was planned out. The Supply Officer had made all the arrangements last week and I had the itinerary memorized. I went over it in my head as I lay in my rack.

I was in a place called the United Arab Emirates. It was over in the Gulf. If you look on a map, it's South of Kuwait. The Gulf War had just "finished," if I can use that term loosely. It was time to transfer to my next duty assignment. I was to attend a new school in Chicago, at the NAVAL Base located in Great Lakes. An Engineering school that would teach me everything there was to know about electronics and Gas Turbine Engines. The school would last for almost two years. I was really excited.

In the morning, there would be a taxi driver standing by to take me to an airport in Fujairah. From there, I would catch a military flight to a place called Abu Dhabi. From Abu Dhabi, I would catch a ride via Italy and then England, to Chicago's O'Hare. And from there, Great Lakes NAVAL Base. Now my hometown is just a hop, skip and a jump from there so I had planned on taking a side trip to visit my family after I settled in. I had 30 days of leave to schedule. Leave is vacation. This would be the longest stretch of vacation I ever took. And I really needed it.

That was it, plain and simple. Right?

As morning time came, I gathered up all my belongings that fit in two sea bags and a garment bag. I headed for the main deck. As I passed all my shipmates, I bade them farewell as they wished me luck. I took a few side trips, there were several guys I would really miss and wanted to make sure I said goodbye to them.

I walked on the main deck and spied my taxi guy. He was sitting on the hood of his mini-van reading a newspaper. He was a native decked out in native gear from flowing robes to the turbine on the head. I yelled out for him with a smile on my face and waved. I raced toward the brow.

Stepping off the ship, I walked straight for him. I looked back one more time at my ship as I saw the sailors pulling the mooring lines away and a tug boat nearby to pull them away from the pier. I closed the distance between the taxi driver and me. Let's call him Mohammad. I really can't remember his name. So Mohammad will do just fine.

I introduced myself to Mohammad and he looked at me with distaste. With a very thick accent, he told me that I was 12 hours late and that his shift was over. He told me I was on my own. Before I could protest, he hopped in his van and off he went. I didn't even have a chance to tell him that there must be some mistake. What a jerk.

Sadly, I turned back around to my ship and noted that all the lines were pulled and she was about 20 feet away from the pier. Now what was I supposed to do? One thing was for certain; I wasn't getting back on the ship, even if I wanted to. I turned around and looked at the pier, really noticing it for the first time. It was a huge parking lot the size of four football fields. I looked back at the ship, now 40 feet away.

Just by chance, I saw the Supply Officer walking by, the one that supposedly made all the arrangements. I hollered out to him and he looked down at me. He cupped his hands to his mouth and yelled, "What the hell are you still doing here?"

I yelled back, explaining the situation. I was a little upset. After hearing it all, the Supply Officer dug in his pants and pulled something out. He threw it at me. I picked it up off the ground and noted that they were a set of keys.

"Do you see that car over there?" the Supply Officer yelled, pointing behind me. I looked back and at the far end of the parking lot was a tiny speck I assumed was a car. Before I could turn around and answer, the Supply Officer yelled, "Take it and find warehouse 8. There will be an American by the name of John that will give you a ride to Fujairah. Good Luck!"

As I turned back toward the ship, the Supply Officer disappeared within the safety of the ship. This was just great, I thought. So I picked up my two sea bags and garment bag and headed toward the car. Mind you that it is over 100 degrees by now. I was already sweating. I must have lost ten pounds just getting to the car. And it was still morning.

Reaching the car, I loaded it up and belted myself in. I didn't know what the rules were on car safety here, but I didn't want to cause trouble. Let me explain...

When we first pulled into the Middle East, my Skipper and several others (including myself) were invited by the constable to view a town trial. We loaded up in the Skipper's Sedan and went to the town square. They were holding "court" sessions there and we witnessed a horror that is absolutely barbaric in nature. Our court system may have some issues to resolve, but it isn't *that* bad. Get this...

We witnessed a man get his hand chopped off for stealing. Another man had his eyes burned out for something I don't even wish to know about, maybe peeping in on a Mullah's harem. I never asked. We witnessed several lashings for minor offenses and finally, an execution. After it was all done, my Skipper turned to the constable and asked why he was showing us this. He replied plainly, "This is what will happen to your men if they get out of line in my country." Enough said, I suppose.

So as you can see, no precaution was too overzealous. The seat belt went on.

Starting the car up, I noticed that I was on "E." That was fitting. I should have realized how much foreshadowing that this was in the trials to follow for me ahead. I accepted it as a logical axiom. Off I went praying that I would have enough gas to find warehouse 8.

Not to my surprise, finding warehouse 8 was quite a challenge. Not only were there tons of warehouses, but also the writing on them was in Arabic. I didn't know which one was which. I stopped at many to no avail. They were all empty, and I wasn't certain how much fume I had left in my car.

I must have visited ten or so warehouses. As I was approaching another, the car started sputtering. I was running out of fumes. This would be my last warehouse before I went searching on foot. Fortunately for me however, it appeared that God was on my side just this once. It was warehouse 8. Excluding all the Arabic stuff written on it, there was also a big 8 on the side. Wow. I was too worn out to be excited.

I just threw the keys in the car, left the door open and left it that way as I walked into the warehouse. Inside was a small office. I walked in. Two natives were there that didn't speak much English. I told them my story but they pretended not to understand me. Then I mentioned the name John. They both shared an inside joke and indicated for me to have a seat. I sat there silently, enjoying the air-conditioner right behind me.

About one hour had passed when finally a trucker came in, rolling his rig to a stop. He came straight to the office. My hero. I stood up and asked if he was John. He indicated yes. I told him my story and that my Supply Officer told me to seek him out for a ride. John sized me up and then asked me how much money I had to offer him. Did I mention to you all that I only had 10 bucks to my name?

I told him I didn't have any money. John turned around in disgust and walked out of the office. I followed John and noticed him jump into a fork truck. He was going to load his semi, I gathered. I approached him again and asked for a moment of his time. I was in desperation mode now.

I offered to load his truck for him if he would give me a ride to Fujairah. He agreed. That is what he probably had in mind all along anyway. So, I hopped in the fork truck and started loading. It took me almost 4 hours.

After the loading was complete, I walked back into the office where John and my two Arabian friends were. By this time, I had my shirt off. I was soaked with sweat, and walking into that air-conditioned room was just plain relief. I paused a moment for breath, then told John we were ready to go. He looked at me in disgust. Apparently, I took too long. I tried to lighten the mood by telling a joke about the temperature. That just seemed to infuriate him more. And now, my two natives looked offended as well. I kept my mouth shut from that moment on and sat down.

John gave me one last sour look before he turned back to the other two to finish the conversation he was having with them in their tongue. I sat patiently. Then he got up and motioned for me to come along. I smiled briefly at the other two and waved good-bye.

We walked out to the rig and John inspected my work. I was an amateur, true, when it came to loading trucks, but John gave me a small smile (the first one ever). Apparently, I did okay. He spent a few minutes changing a few things around and securing the load. Then he closed the back doors and locked them in place. We were ready to go.

We jumped into the cab and off we went. My partner and I pretty much kept our thoughts to ourselves for the first hour. I was content just looking at all the sand as we drove down a lonely piece of road. Let me tell you, there is a drive you can make in the United States from East to West through Southern Utah. If you've ever made that drive, you know that it is truly no man's land. There is absolutely nothing but sand and rock. This was the same drive, without the rock.

If I can take this time out and tell you about something else I have learned in life while taking this road trip. This one is simple and will only come useful to you maybe just once in your life. You may find it in a Trivial Pursuit game, you may find yourself on Jeopardy and are asked this. It may even be a simple question on an exam in school for extra credit. Or, more likely, it may just be a small piece of worthless nothing that opens the door for conversation with someone you are trying to break the ice with. But, in any event and for what it is worth, here it is, just something I have noted. The ugliest animal in the world (next to a sharpe' pig) is a Dubai Goat. They were everywhere. And they are the foulest things...

About halfway into our trip to Fujairah, we pulled into the town of Dubai. It was very small and in the middle of nowhere. John stopped his rig and turned to me. He said he was going to get something to eat and asked if I wanted anything. I was hungry and hadn't eaten all day. I recalled that $10 was all I had, so I regretfully declined. I hunched down and closed my eyes as John walked out of the rig. I fell into a troublesome, half sleep.

I woke up to the sound of John opening the door. I looked down at his clock. He was gone for two hours. I looked at him. He looked like he just ran a marathon. He looked at me with a sheepish grin. He didn't get something to eat at all; he was visiting a woman, intimately. What a gross waste of time for me. It was then that I realized I was probably late for my flight in Fujairah. I didn't say a word. I'll worry about my flight when I get there.

Silence was the main topic when we left and drove for about an hour and a half more to finally reach our destination to the Fujairah airport. It was about 18:00. Relief washed over me. But now wasn't the time to relax. That was just one hurdle. I knew I had many more to come before I would finally arrive home safely.

We entered the airport area on the southeast corner; the only thing visible was a small building whose view blocked the rest of the airport. John rolled to a stop. He pointed to the building and said that's where I wanted to be. I bade him farewell and jumped out of the truck.

Grabbing both my sea bags and garment bag, I walked into the building, hoping it was air-conditioned. When I entered, I noticed three gentlemen in civilian clothes acknowledge me. I placed my items down on the floor, pulled out my Military I.D. card and introduced myself. I told them my story, that I was Joseph C. Powell and here to catch a flight to Abu Dhabi. They looked at me confused and told me that they had no idea what I was talking about. There should be a law in life that states life should not be interrupted by hurdles so close to one another. Sometimes you just need to take a break from them. Don't you think?

It didn't take me long to figure out that these folks were from the Air Force. Their job was to send items from this part of overseas to the U.S. and vice versa through the postal system. It didn't take them long to figure out that I was in the NAVY. At that point, understanding entered their eyes. Finally, some good news I thought. They told me that the NAVY has a little shop here too. It was right behind the building I was in. I just didn't see it when we arrived here. They told me that trailer is where I wanted to be. The folks there would surely know what to do with me. I thanked them and they wished me good luck as I left. While walking out, they were right behind me. It was time for them to go home too.

I walked behind the building, which brought the whole airport into view. The Air Force building was in the southeast section. I looked at the airport terminal itself. It was separated by the Air Force's building with the one airstrip itself, which looked about a football field in width. It was closed down for the night. I turned to the left and saw the Navy building. It was actually a small trailer. I walked up to it. Going to the front door, I saw the sign that said "Closed, be back tomorrow at 08:00." Ok, what's new? So I walked back to the Air Force building. They indeed closed up shop and left. Then I walked to the airport terminal. It took me 15 minutes to cross the landing strip. It indeed was closed as well.

So I walked back to the NAVY trailer. There was a park bench on the side. I placed my three items on the sand and sat down on the bench. I had 12 hours to kill with nothing to do. It took me just a short time to figure this one out so, using one of my sea bags as a pillow; I lay down on the picnic table and tried to get some sleep. It took some time for it to finally arrive. It was getting very cold out. But eventually, sleep came.

I had a dream of being in a fire. It was extremely hot. The billowing smoke filling my lungs. I was choking. The heat from the fire prickling my skin. Like all dreams, at the unpredicted end, I awoke. I slowly opened my eyes, forgetting were I was. And then, I realized it was no dream at all!

As my eyes opened, I heard someone whisper, "Shhh. Stay perfectly still. Do not move. Don't even breathe..." I closed my eyes again for a moment only, and then reopened them. The smoke was thick.

At the corner of my eye, I could see at least two gentlemen waving firebrands slowly over my body. Just then, I remembered where I was. I could feel something crawling all over me. A lot of little things crawling all over me. Taking a chance, I turned my head slowly to the side and looked down at my body. Scorpions were all over me, scurrying away from the faggots of fire and smoke. I remained perfectly still.

Moving only my eyeballs this time, I peered up at one of my benefactors. Though in civilian clothes, I could tell this was a fellow shipmate. I figured these guys knew what they were doing. He looked down at me while waving his torches over my body. He smiled at me and said again, "Stay still, a couple stings and you're not going home alive, I promise you that." The only thing I could think of at that moment was how in the world could that possibly have been said with a smile?

It is very difficult to resist the urge to jump up when you have all these creatures crawling all over you. But still, I remained. The smoke trick was working. The scorpions were jumping off of me at an alarming rate. It only took a few minutes before all of them were off of me. All but one at least.

When the coast was clear, my shipmates told me to get up. So I did. I looked down and saw DOZENS of scorpions scurrying away. That's probably exaggerating but, I wouldn't be surprised if it was half that many. I finally was able to speak. "Thank you" was all I could spit out though.

My rescuers told me that I was lucky. Here in the desert, it gets cold at night and any live body is the only source of heat for miles around. Scorpions are attracted to that. As I camped out on the bench, they camped out on me. I wondered how long they were on me. They told me that if I was here all night, they were probably on me for just as long. Any tossing or turning, loud snoring, anything of that ilk, and I would never have awoken from that last night of sleep. I don't know if that was true or not, but I was lucky indeed.

So, sitting on the bench with the two beside me, I calmed down and told them who I was. They indicated for me to come inside the trailer. As

I got up, I grabbed my two sea bags and garment bag and proceeded to follow them inside. That's when I felt it. The "lone wolf" on my ankle. I stopped in my tracks. But before I could do anything about it, the scorpion jumped off of me, but not without a little kiss. He stung me on the back of my ankle and scurried away. I thought about squishing him with my boot, but live and let live right? Hogwash, I love animals but I needed a little taste of success, just as much as the scorpion needed a taste of my heel. But before I could exact my revenge, he scurried under a large rock. I couldn't even win that battle. I knew that one little sting wasn't going to kill me, but I was worried about getting sick from the poison. I turned around and followed my buddies inside.

I won't go into much more detail about the sting than this: it was a miserable experience. I didn't see a doctor; I didn't have it attended to until a week later. I didn't start feeling the effects until some 12 hours later. I developed what's called Cellulitis and my ankle swelled up to the size of a softball. It took a month for it to heal. Fifteen years later, I still have the hole in my ankle. Enough said there.

The two sailors that ran the operation here looked at their itinerary and knew who I was. They looked up at me and said, "Shipmate, you're a little late." That was obvious. I asked them what I needed to do now. They told me that they have a Military Flight going to Abu Dhabi at 16:00 and that I was more than welcome to hang around until then. Like I had any choice.

They had a small library there for occasions just like this that comprised of 200 or so books, none of which were more than 200 pages deep. They ran from Harlequins to Reader's Digests. Nothing interesting. I must have read about half of them. I'm embarrassed to say that I have resorted to reading this trash (no offense to the companies of course, but I'm sure they couldn't argue with me), but there really wasn't much else to do. Or was there?

At around 14:00, I stood up and walked over to my buddies. I asked them if I could use their phone to call home. Surprisingly enough, they told me that all the phones here and at the Air Force building couldn't reach overseas. They told me that if I wanted to make a call, I'd have to go to the airport's terminal. They told me to take my sea bags with me. Sometimes when they leave the trailer, the locals come out of nowhere, break into the trailer, and steal whatever they can get their hands on. I noticed their collection of books once more.

Not asking "how," I picked up my stuff and commenced the long trek to the terminal. It was so hot out and I'm going on my second day without a shower. I'm sure I was becoming offensive to even a Dubai goat.

About halfway across the run strip, a white, and VERY expensive-looking jet came rolling to a stop right in front of me. When it made its last inch, the door opened and the ladder extended itself. Turning slightly to the left to give the jet a little distance, I proceeded forward.

The terminal doors opened up and I saw some "Hasheeb" guy walking out with flowing robes, a habit-looking headdress and about ten armed guards. They spied me within seconds. Not really realizing what was happening, two of the guards grabbed the guy in white and rushed him back to the terminal while the rest locked and loaded on me. They were sporting machine guns.

I dropped everything I had, put my hands in the air and said "What?" I was a little numb at this point with everything that had transpired over the past two days. I wasn't surprised at all. The guards started for me quickly, guns at the ready, screaming at me in their own tongue. I thought of the TV show *Cops*. The policemen on that show are always telling the bad guys to get on their bellies. So that's what I proceeded to do. Who says TV isn't real? Getting on one knee, I calmly stated that I speak English. They were very close to me now.

By the time I was on both knees, they had bridged the remaining gap and one spoke to me in English. "Are you American?"

I stopped and looked up. "Yes, sir, and apparently, an unwise one. What have I done?" I spoke to him in a sour tone.

The armed guard that spoke up looked at me and smiled. I was happy for that, not many people have smiled as of late around here. While on my knee, he spoke to me in a thick accent and explained to me the error of my ways. I really can't say word for word what he said, quite frankly, it was 13 years ago and I just can't remember. But here's the content...

The United Arab Emirates is governed by "Seven Princes of the Royal Crown". My good man with the habit was one of them. By walking within 100 feet of him without permission as a soldier of a foreign nation, I have violated an international peace treaty. Some sort of "territorial bubble" so to speak. The soldiers had the right to shoot me on sight. I am, however, slightly gratified that they gave me a little latitude. I wasn't ready to die; I wanted that 30 days of vacation first at the very least.

I explained to the man my humble experiences that brought me to this point and then we made a deal. I would remain on my knees with the machine guns at the ready. As long as I didn't move, and after the prince boarded the jet and in the air, they would then let me leave. Fair enough.

After the jet took off, and true to their word, I was free to go. I picked up my belongings, and walked into the airport. It was pretty much empty with the exception of a few workers. They all stared at me with amusement. I ignored them and went straight to a pay phone and dialed home.

I only had that $10 on me and wasn't ready to spend it, so my call was collect. Remember, I have ten siblings. I tried reaching them all. Answering machines are all I got. I've grown to dislike answering machines while overseas. You can't leave a message calling collect. I'd sit there for an hour letting the phone ring until someone picks up if I could. But with an answering machine, you only get about 5 rings.

Discouraged, I left the airport's terminal and, looking out for jets, I walked back to the NAVY trailer. My flight would arrive soon. I wasn't going to miss this one. Stepping into the trailer, my benefactors told me they saw the whole thing. They said I was lucky to be alive. That's the second time they told me that. I was on a roll I suppose. I told them that life has a way of working things out. I thought a moment for the first time about the scorpion sting. I thought about telling them but, foolishly, thought if I did, they would cancel my flight and send me to the hospital. If one existed out here, that is. All I wanted to do was get home. I kept my mouth shut.

The flight arrived on the hour. I was anxious to begin the next leg of my journey. Shortly after it landed, I helped the two sailors load it up with mail and whatnots, and then I boarded it myself. This was going to be the coolest flight of my life. I don't think most people would enjoy this but, for me, it was a blast.

There were a dozen or so seats all facing the back of the plane, which bottom opened up to the outside. Sort of like a "ramp" that functioned as a "door." I buckled up my seat, which was more like a harness strap that covered the whole torso. You see, that ramp would never close. As the plane took off, it went into a 45-degree angle upward. I was facing the ground as it slowly shrank with the aircraft's ascent. The only regret I have is that I didn't choose the back (front) seat for a better view.

A short time later, we landed on an Army's air base. It was here that I would catch a flight back to the States. I was happy to be around Americans once again. I love all people, but I needed a short break from the foreign lifestyle. After leaving the plane, I was directed to go to a place called SATO on base. They were to have prepared for me a flight to the United States. I was late, but I was certain they could find me something.

Now, it was the middle of December, everyone American in the Middle East going home for the holidays were going through this place. I didn't realize it until a few moments later that a flight would be difficult to find. I walked into SATO and introduced myself.

They told me that there currently weren't any free flights but to keep checking every day. I didn't want to stay here. I told them that I was under orders but it still didn't change anything. They told me that there are about twenty other people awaiting flights. I would have to wait my turn. In the meantime, they told me (and gave me directions to) a hotel on base where I could stay free of charge until a flight was captured for me. I went to the hotel.

Walking in, I went straight to the counter and introduced myself. I explained to them who I was and why I was there. I told them that SATO had sent me and said I could stay until a flight was arranged. At this point in my journey, it didn't come to a surprise to me when they said I couldn't have a room until they see reservations for a flight. I went back to SATO.

SATO told me that the hotel was being silly and to go back and get a room. I went back to the hotel and told them that they were silly; they sent me back to SATO. At this time, the twenty or so military personnel that were also having the same problems were feeling my discouragement. Back and forth all of us went like ants from SATO to hotel until eventually, the SATO closed up shop for the night. We had no choice but to just "hang out."

In retaliation, we camped out on the sidewalk right in front of the hotel and spent the night there. I made sure to cover myself well. I was starting to feel the nauseating sickness of the scorpion sting.

No one seemed to care that we were on the sidewalk. Apparently, the base has seen this sort of behavior many times before. That's an Army base for you. We were camped out for three nights.

On the fourth day, I walked into SATO ready to be a rebel. Something you just don't do in the military. I was in the NAVY though; we got away with that kind of stuff easier than the other services. Our reputation as being drunken partiers does have its privileges, don't you know?

I walked up to the counter and told the people there that my body has not seen water for five or so days now. If they did not get me into that hotel for a shower and a flight, both in that order, then I would sit there and stink up the whole place until they did so. I don't know if it was pity or their belief in my threat, but they had both waiting for me. A flight was scheduled and would take me home in 14 hours.

I would hop on a military Boeing, make a short stop in Sicily, head to Heathrow airport in London, hop a Concord to Chicago, and get this, I had a connecting flight to my hometown. Things started to look bright for me. And with reservations in hand, I walked to the hotel demanding a room.

My shower lasted an hour. It was pure bliss. The only thing better at that point was the bed. I usually only need four or five hours of sleep, but that day I slept for ten. It seemed only a moment had passed when the alarm rang. Two hours till my flight.

I took another shower, put on fresh clothes and went back to SATO. From there, they taxied me to the airstrip and I boarded my plane. Everything after that was pretty much downhill from there. I had a couple more challenges ahead of me before reaching home though.

Landing in Italy was uneventful; I left the plane to board another and shortly thereafter, was in the air again headed for London. Once reaching London's Heathrow airport, I walked to the terminal were my next flight would take me to the States. Once there, I looked at the clock and noted that I had half an hour before boarding. I decided to go get a book with my VISA card. And stood up and began to walk out of the terminal.

The lady at the counter stopped me. She told me that security was tight and that they usually don't allow passengers to leave without good reason and not without rendering their passport. I explained to her that all I wanted to do was get a book, it would be a long flight to the states, and that all I had on me was my Military ID card, which in fact dubbed as a passport. But I couldn't give THAT to her. She told me "No," then. I went back to my seat, sulking like a child. All I wanted was a darn book.

She must have felt sorry for me. She approached me a few moments later and told me that I looked innocent enough (she didn't know I was a sailor) and that I could go get a book as long as I hurried back and didn't get into any trouble. I can do that, right?

Not more than 50 feet out of the terminal and I was already setting off alarms, and the guards. What now? I was ready to get on my knees again when the guards approached and asked me to follow them. They took my two sea bags and garment bag. We walked into an "alcove" of sorts and they frisked me. Other guards were going through my stuff looking for *airport no-nos*. You know, bombs and such.

I opened my mouth for the first time and they realized I was American. I won't go through the entire dialog but what became apparent to me is this: Heathrow is an airport shaped somewhat like a circle. You can only travel in a clockwise fashion. Failure to do that results in what was happening to me right now. I failed to do that. When they realized I was clean, they told me to go back to the terminal and behave myself. I looked up at the clock. The plane should have left by now. I told them this. They informed me that the counter would be able to arrange another flight. I would have to use my VISA now. I was in the civilian world. I was on my own now.

Like a child caught in the cookie jar, I approached the lady at the counter with the most innocent look I could give. "I told you not to get in any trouble." She told me, "But you're in luck, your flight was delayed. They're boarding now. Hurry up now, go catch your flight, and do try and stay out of trouble from now on."

Well, there is a God after all. I boarded the Concord just in time. Up to this point, everything was quite uneventful except for the small trip from Chicago to my hometown; which was a bit miserable. If it wasn't for that Chief of mine on the first ship I was on (in Guam) I probably would have made a fool of myself. Well, actually, I did make a fool of myself. But I did manage to salvage a bit of my dignity.

While waiting for my flight in O'Hare that would take me home, I went to the bar and fixed myself a large cup of coffee. I would be home soon, but I was getting very sleepy. My family would keep me up late, so I wanted to perk up a bit.

By the time I tossed most of the coffee down my gullet, it was time to board the aircraft. I sat next to a nice old lady and we shared some small talk before lapsing into that robot mode that people tend to gravitate toward on aircrafts.

About half way in our trip home, the coffee started to work its magic on me. I had to go. I wasn't in "crisis" mode yet, but why wait. We were at cruising altitude, so I unbuckled myself and went to the back of the plane to find the restroom. It wasn't there. I walked to the front of the plane, none there either. I looked around for someone to help.

The only stewardess on the craft saw my confusion and approached me asking if she could help me out. I asked her where the bathroom was. To my shock, she said there wasn't any. I went back to my seat. It was at this time I thought of my old Chief...

One day, while standing watch, late at night in the Engineering plant on my first ship, I had to use the restroom. I went to my Chief, who also was on watch, and asked if I could step out to take care of it. He told me something that inadvertently helped me this day. He said, "Powell, I'm going to teach you a lesson in restraint. I'm going to teach you how to hold your bladder. No, you cannot leave." I was dismayed. The Chief made me wait to the end of the watch before I could use the restroom.

So, here I am on the aircraft, about half an hour to go before we reach our destination, another 15 minutes to land and probably an additional 15 minutes to stop for debarkation. No sweat. I sat patiently. Concentrating hard on controlling my bladder.

By the time we reached home, the pilot got on the horn and told us that there would be a delay in landing due to the heavy traffic and weather. He estimated that it would be an hour before we could land. I started to panic quietly inside.

Now this little old lady is right next to me so I can't play with myself to relieve the pressure (a guy secret), but I am doing the little dance routine with my legs. I really had to go bad now. I was in that delirious phase were peeing your pants actually seemed OK to do. I even thought about hiding in the back and peeing in my coffee cup.

Since I was now delirious, I got up once again and went straight to the cabin. I walked in on both pilots. Sadly enough, I was belligerent. They looked at me in shock, but I was in uniform so they gave me pause. I told them that if they do not land this plane now, I was going to mark my territory all over their plane. They became just as belligerent and told me to go back to my seat. Energy spent, I went back to sit down.

I looked at my coffee cup again with a gleam in my eye, then the little old lady patted me on the knee and said "Don't worry, I know how you feel. I have a bladder problem too." That was it! I grabbed my coffee cup and was ready to get up.

Then, the pilot got on the horn again and said they had good news. They were clear for landing. That gave me a small measure of strength. I sat back down, put on my seatbelt and started concentrating again.

Once we landed and were at the gate, I thought to myself that not all was lost. I was still able to maintain a shred of my dignity. I made a fool of myself with this little old lady and the crew, but at least I didn't pee my pants. It would only be moments before the doors opened and I could go to the bathroom. Just a little dignity left. That was enough.

When the ground crew started to bring in the ladder for us to disembark, the Skipper got on the horn one last time to speak to the ground crew. "Hey you guys, hurry up out there, we have a sailor on board that is about to piss his pants!"

At that point, all eyes turned to me. I just lost that shred of dignity. I was so embarrassed. It would be okay to pee my pants now. I've got nothing to lose. However, the Chief popped in my head again. "Restraint," he had said on that quiet night of training.

Once the ladder was in place, everyone was more than happy to let me out first. I never felt better in my entire life than at that moment at the urinal. Thanks, Chief. I'm home now. It was time to start thinking about the doctor. Truly for the first time, I was concerned about the little pain in my ankle.

# Chapter 5

We pulled into Australia after an extended stint in the South Pacific. I was really excited at this point. Ever since I joined the NAVY, I heard the stories about her from every sailor who has ever been there. All the stories were the same. The people are friendly; they love American sailors, nine women for every man. It was a paradise. I heard this from everyone. Sailors will actually reenlist just for the *opportunity* to go to Australia. And here it is, five years later; I will be making my first of four trips to the continent.

The first night there, several shipmates and I had three days to play before we had to report back for duty. So with pockets full of cash, we left the ship with only one idea in mind.... What kind of trouble can we get into? And subsequently get out of, without our ship finding out. Now, sailors aren't bad people, quite enjoyable actually for the most part. We just like getting into mischief. It can be very therapeutic at times. Ask the people I work with now. I'm nothing but trouble.

It was late in the morning so we figured that it was appropriate to start drinking. 12:00 is the respectable time, so we decided to head to a nice restaurant and discuss what we were going to do for the next two and half days.

While eating, we had our waitress keep us company by telling us all the things in the area we could do. None of it really sounded interesting. All the suggestions she gave us were things we could do in America. Then she told us about *Walk-About* or *Boonie-Stomping* in the Bush. Something popular I suppose in this neck of the woods. To put it simply, you just grab a vehicle and go explore. That's what we decided to do.

We invited her to come along but unfortunately, her boyfriend wouldn't approve. Can't understand why. Do you see anything wrong with a young lady disappearing for three days with five sailors that have been out to sea for about 45 days? We surely couldn't.

After brunch, we went to the local rent-a-car establishment and rented a nice jeep with a *Roo-Bar* and took off into the Bush. We traveled for perhaps an hour before we found open land and went into the desert. We drove for a couple hours, stopping every so often to take pictures and explore. Then, we came across a pack of red kangaroos.

We had the old American thought that kangaroos are these cute cuddly things, until we approached them. I have found a new respect for these animals. The reds can stand up to six or so feet tall. They have sharp claws on hinds and front three inches long and fairly sharp. Their tails, which act as a third leg, are extremely well muscled and can kill. In a confrontation, they will support themselves on their tails, hold on to their victims with their front claws, and gouge with their hind ones. Docile creatures, but you wouldn't want to anger them. Well, that's exactly what this one fellow did with us. I'll refer to him as Tad.

Let me tell you about Tad. Every ship has one. He was one of those drugstore cowboys from Oklahoma who wore a belt buckle as big as his head and a cowboy hat big enough to swim in. He had a cheap western drawl that would make Hank W. Jr. roll in his grave. This guy thought he was John Wayne, and he was as sharp as a bowling ball.

All this comic relief you can almost deal with. What was difficult to tolerate is that this guy never brushed his teeth (because it made his gums bleed, he would explain) and never took a bath. I swear the man couldn't even spell bath. Flies were afraid of him.

He stunk, plain and simple. I used to work at a zoo when I was in high school and never have I smelled an animal's one-week-old-urine-soaked straw more offensive than Tad. He was quite offensive. About once per week we had to ask our Chief to tell Tad to take a bath. He would never do it on his own. On top of that, he had an I.Q. that would only impress a gold fish. I have no idea how he got in the NAVY. But like I said, every ship has one. I suppose some recruiters are more desperate than others.

Anyway, he violated these kangaroos in the worst way.

Once we stopped, we exited the jeep and approached the roost carefully; they were just hanging around, digging things up. We had some food on us, some puffed rice cereal, so I grabbed the box and I brought it with me. Coming up to a kangaroo that was hunched over, I pulled out some of my cereal.

He looked up at me, but was still hunched over. I came closer. Putting the cereal in the palm of my hand, I reached out to the kangaroo. He closed the distance and stood up.... and up.... and up... to his full height of seven feet. His two front claws were on my shoulders; he was peering down at me. I looked up and down the length of this beast, that's when I noticed how big they really were, how dangerous their claws could be, how powerful their tail actually was. I also noted that his testicles were unnaturally huge. (You had to be there).

I looked back up at him; I didn't seem to be in immediate danger. I offered my cereal to him. He began to eat out of my hand. He finished it in short order so I pulled out some more. He really liked it. He didn't seem that dangerous to me after all. I pulled out the whole box of cereal now.

All of a sudden, Tad, the guy with the Garth Brooks starter kit, came up from behind the kangaroo and kicked him in the testicles. I went very, very still. I was, after all, about ready to die now. I felt the roo's front claws dig a little too deep into my shoulders. The roo looked back at Tad. He was just grinning as if he did something hilarious. All my other shipmates stopped what they were doing and told Tad quietly that he just killed me.

I kept silent. The roo looked back down at me and began to eat the cereal again. I looked over at Tad with fear in my eyes, cautioning him to just get away. He had a confused look on his face now. Then he smiled again and gave the roo another swift kick, much harder this time. Truly an idiot.

The roo gave out a yelp and all the other kangaroos became agitated. They began to converge on Tad and me. The roo holding onto me let go. At that point, I dropped all my cereal on the ground, did a drop-roll, vaulted up and ran to the jeep as fast as I could.

The offended roo reared himself to Tad, who just stood there like a brave little cowboy. The roo stood on his tail, ready to strike. At that point, all the other sailors were in the jeep and we started it. At the sound of the engine turning over, all the roos stopped and looked our way. I think in fear, but the reaction was momentary. That's all the time the idiot needed to escape to the jeep.

Once all members were in the vehicle, we took off into the desert. We could only go about 60 miles per hour, the kangaroos were following us, and they were relentless. But eventually, machine prevailed over beast as we slowly watched the roos disappear in the horizon. Every one of us simultaneously chastised Tad for being such a moron. I think he was too stupid to realize what had just happened.

After a short period of time, we came across a watering hole. It was small and clear. You could see to the bottom. No crocs here. It was hot so we decided to go for a swim, you could see the fear in Tad's eyes. We made him come with us. So, we stripped off our clothes and dove in. It was wonderful. The water was about 70 degrees and crystal clear. No wildlife that our eyes could see. As a matter of fact, there wasn't life anywhere that we could see.

No trees, no fish, not even the sound of a dingo. But before I could mention this fact out loud to my troops, they came. Those kangaroos faithfully followed us to this watering hole. There they were, camped out on the shore where our clothes were. None of us wanted to come out of the water. They might have still been angry. So there we waited, and it was getting dark.

For the years to come, all of us fondly tell this story saying that the kangaroos hunted us down. But if I were to think of this logically, being nomadic in nature, these roos probably knew about this watering hole and visited it from time to time to quench their thirst. You need to do that every once in a while in the desert. You really have no choice.

Right before the last rays of sun disappeared, another nomadic tribe came by. This one was human. Aborigines. They took a look at us and saw immediately that we were hiding from the roos so they chased off the beasts with fire, sticks and rocks.

They probably saved our lives. As long as the animals stayed, we would have stayed in the water. But the natives were successful in frightening them away. They looked at us and laughed. Timidly, we left the water and put on our clothes. We all looked at Tad and two of us, in stereo, told him that if he opened his mouth or did any action, we would personally skin him alive. He was smart enough to acknowledge. We didn't know how hostile they could be and we didn't wish to take any chances. I silently promised myself never to have Tad come along again.

It turned out that these natives were about the friendliest, English-speaking people I have ever met. They actually weren't nomadic at all. They had jobs and family in Sydney, but on some weekends they would all get together, throw on their aboriginal gear and do a walk-a-bout like their ancestors used to do. They invited us to join them.

We jumped on that opportunity. We painted ourselves like them, and ate bats and grubs. And over the course of the next couple of days, they taught us how to use boomerangs as hunting tools, dig for water, and start fires. I tell you what, that show *Survivor* can't give me anything I can't handle. We had a blast.

One of the natives with us owned a souvenir shop. He made most of his stuff too. Currently, he, as well as the whole group, was making boomerangs. We, always so helpful, made a few for him also. Not very good quality, I would like to remind you. I think he threw them away... But, he did make a couple for me. I still have them. They are a work of art, really.

At night, we had to post sentries to look out for dingoes. Dingoes are scavengers mostly, they explained, but will hunt also. They feared our campfires though and generally left us alone. We never really had problems with them except for the occasional stray that required almost no effort to scare away.

We took turns on those watches. When it was my turn late at night, I would sit up on a large rock and look up at the stars, nothing more beautiful. I had a great time. We always stood the watches in pairs. The native that stood watch with me, his name was George, would tell me stories of folklore and myth of his country. I would love to share some of those with you but I made a promise to him.

I told him that one day, I would write a book on my experiences in the NAVY. I told him that he should do the same with his stories. So I promised him that I would not touch his stories if he promised to write them down and publish it. I have yet to find his book if he indeed wrote it, but a man's only as good as his word. If you ever come across a book by a guy named "Sir George", that's the one.

# Chapter 6

I left Mayport, Florida and spent one week crossing the Atlantic. After the first nine days or so, I arrived at the Straights of Gibraltar. I was surprised to see that this Prudential icon actually has a city on it. We were not scheduled to make a stop there, to my disappointment. But we encountered a snag during our sea detail. One of our emergency diesel generators decided to be finicky that day so we had to park the ship just less than 24 hours for repairs. This afforded some of us time to charter a small boat and take us to the rock.

One day later found me in Palma De Mallorca (Majorca, never really could get that right), which is a Spanish island just inside the Mediterranean ocean, one of the Balearic Islands. I rented a car for two days to jaunt the island. I visited Bellver castle, which was built by the Romans during their great empire, ran by the Arabs and then, later, became a haven for Hindu monks.

The entrance to the castle was a series of warn stone steps that ascended its way to the top of the small mountain from which the castle adorned its apex. It took me at least thirty minutes to climb up there. I was under the assumption that I was in pretty good shape. I had to give this careful consideration once I reached the top, however.

Once there, I found to my disappointment that it was a major tourist trap that required about 500 pesetas just to get in. So like any tourist, I paid it and walked inside. There was a huge crowd of people gathered there. I had a few buddies with me as well. But the place was large enough to where you felt *alone*, allowing yourself to lose track of time and space. We spent the whole morning there.

My first sight upon entering the castle grounds was the awesome depth of the moat. It was approximately 150 feet deep and 75 feet wide. I tried to imagine how much water it took to fill her, and what it harbored in its depths. But for that matter, how do you suppose they filled it with water in the first place? I had no idea.

As I entered the castle, I was greeted by a courtyard, which covered most of the castle grounds and was exposed to the sky. A cursory glance revealed a well off-centered in the middle of the yard and statues off to the side. I went for a quick browse inside. Instead of visiting the various rooms, I just climbed the steps and found myself on the roof. Immediately, I spied a parapet and climbed it to observe the grounds, and the mountain in which it sat, and the city, and the ocean beyond.

As I stood there, I imagined what it must have been like for the Roman, and later, Spanish soldier that stood watch on the very parapet in which I stood. I closed my eyes but could still see the mountain, the town, the ocean with the faint sound of sea birds singing their lonely songs…

*He must have carried a bow unstrung with a quiver at his side. And he watched. Though his life was much simpler, he was not any different from me, standing there at night while others slept, So others Could sleep. The sacrifice for a just purpose, and he watched.*

*He had a family I am certain, that worried for him. Prayed for him, just as I do. Was he prideful? Was he lonely and tired? Was he scared? It does not matter, he still watched, we still watched.*

I opened my eyes and found that the sun had traveled some distance across the sky. My shipmates had left on their own accord to experience other areas of the castle no doubt. I descended the stairs to the second level and started entering each room for investigation. Each chamber was a barren stone room with old Roman or Spanish statues or relics on display. Money, pottery, tokens of ages long gone.

I arrived to a locked room and was curious as to what was inside. I stepped out on the balcony of its neighboring room and found that it was connected to the locked room. I peered in the window and saw that it was the throne room. I went to the room opposite the first and found its door to the throne room locked as well. I sat down to think on a way to get inside and the thought came to me: windows.

It did not take long to climb out one and climb into the other for they did not make windows with glass panes back then. I certainly did not wish to be caught, so instead of wandering around, I selected a seat on the dais to the fireplace, which was well hidden from view, and observed.

The throne sat on a dais itself and was scarcely adorned. It was red and tall-backed. Again, I closed my eyes, and could almost hear the courts in session, dukes paying respects to their king. The courtiers whispering gossip off to the side; and the fireplace…

Music? It was the song of the monks, I think; coming from the fireplace, from somewhere up above. I would almost call it a chant, but for the faint changes in pitch to their baritone voices. It was beautiful, how can I explain it. Listening to the music, I felt like I was on top of a mountain overlooking others and the presence of God was near. It made me feel very small, but very alive! It was more than likely a recording, but I had to go find out myself.

After climbing through windows once more, I searched for the stairs and ascended them to the third floor. The whole level of this castle was devoted to the monks and their histories. I found that the music really was just a recording, but it was still wonderful, nonetheless. It was dark. The only light came from the illuminations on the artifacts that the chamber displayed. The setting was so profound that it took you back several centuries to the phenomenal life of that order.

Everything was written in the Spanish Catalan Language, so the only feel I could get had to come from sight and imagination. They displayed all the Hindu artifacts in their glass tombs. Each mask, statue and painting was a setting of unreal images so other-worldly, so different, each a vision of color and shaped horror, it was a surprise to me to find that through what little I could read, that many of the things I saw were a replica of normally peaceful gods.

I browsed for what seemed like minutes, but at the end I knew that hours more had passed. I remembered my shipmates and wondered where they were. I took a brief scan around the castle and could not find them anywhere. I found myself in the courtyard once again and sat down to relax on an old, weatherworn cannon. Sitting off to the side. In the game of hide-and-seek, when you are "it," it is best to stay and wait while others you search for come to you. Once again, I closed my eyes.

I imagined what the courtyard must have been like during the days the Spaniards occupied the castle. The chambermaids carrying their empty jugs to the well for filling and gossiping while courtiers played their politics and the bustle of servants running loose to perform some self-important charge.

And the children playing…

I opened my eyes and turned my head. I was astounded to see what I saw while thinking of the children. It was graffiti. Even back then, we couldn't control them. It was a drawing rather, from a child depicting the very castle I was in. The sun was affixed on top and a dragon loomed in the background. To preserve the drawing, the proprietors of the castle placed a plexiglass cover over it.

There still was no sign of my companions. I made another quick tour around the castle and still could not find them. I walked out to the battlements by the main gate to see if they were there. They were.

They had walked out of the main gate and the guard there would not let them back in unless they paid again. But they also told me that they had not been waiting too long, so I did not feel guilty by asking them to wait just a few moments more. There was one thing left to see. Every castle has a dungeon.

You have to see the dungeon. I'm sure some of you would understand. Now I could not remember seeing anything that remotely resembled the entrance to the dungeon, but knew one had to exist somewhere. If nothing else supported it, the very depth of the moat was a sure giveaway. It was my impression that dungeons would not be the ideal place to show tourists you wished to impress. They must have had it secured from the general public. But I had an idea.

Steeling my courage, I entered the office. There was an older man, probably in his fifties, sitting at a desk and he looked up and smiled when he saw me, "Can I help you?" (He spoke English!)

"Pardon me, sir. I can't help but compliment you on your wonderful castle (a nod of thanks). It is the best I have seen in my tours. Allow me to introduce myself. My name is Todd Muller, and I am an undergraduate student of castle lore at Cambridge University with an endorsement on architectural structure." Frankly, I didn't even know if that made sense or not. But it sounded good.

On a roll, I continued on. "I am doing a thesis on Spanish castles and have visited ten in the past several weeks. This castle, "your" castle, is by far the most impressive. I would like to base the majority of my paper on it. However, I do not feel as if I have fully experienced her unless I am permitted to survey the dungeon."

Looking at me with a bit of skepticism he replied, "We do not generally allow people to see the dungeon sir." He told me this with an air of indifference.

I couldn't stop here, so I countered with, "I do not feel I can completely honor her properly without at least a small peek. I would be eternally grateful." We both stood there, staring at each other for a moment or two. Waiting to see who would speak next.

With a resigning nod of his head, he reluctantly decided to let me have that peek. He motioned for me, with a wave of his hand, to a door behind his desk. I eagerly followed with a thankful smile on my face. Whoever said lying gets you nowhere?

The dungeon lay beyond. I wanted him to leave me alone for a while, but he would have none of it. I kept my peace; I did not wish to press my luck. The dungeon was relatively small. It contained only several cells and only two still had their bars installed. Now it is being used as a storage area, but I can only imagine what it was like when its first purpose was implemented.

I was fairly disappointed at how unmoving the dungeon was. But what did I expect? Torture devices and bones locked to shackles on the wall? I guess I was just being silly. So, after making a minor show of inspecting the way the stones were laid (I had no idea what I was doing), I was ready to leave. I thanked the man and left hurriedly to rejoin my companions.

We left the castle and went to dinner at a very nice restaurant, then returned back to the ship.

On the second day, we left early and drove down to a place called Magaluf for breakfast. We found a nice restaurant on the beach, sat down and ordered. There were many nice things to look at. The beach, ocean, rising sun, coral reefs, naked…(???)

I could not believe it though I kept my surprise in remission. The fat lady sitting two tables down from me took off her shirt (the only article of clothing she wore) and displayed her gargantuan girth to the public, and me. I thought that was very rude. I almost lost my appetite. For those that know me, realize just how difficult that is to achieve.

She left her table and thundered down to the beach where sand met the sea and SPLASH! (Not that I was really watching in the first place). The sea will never be the same to me again. Well, sorry for being so callous.

Anyway, after breakfast, my friends and I toured the town of Magaluf for sightseeing and shopping. Afterwards, we toured part of the island itself to see the sights. It is a glorious island with mountains all over. The constant rush of the ocean was ever present in my ears. But not many people around. I wondered why.

We arrived back at the ship around 17:00 to drop off the car and then take a taxi to Palma to enjoy the cities nightlife. As we arrived, the Executive Officer and the Chief Engineer came to me on the pier and explained about a problem that just occurred within the Engineering Plant. Our Command for Pitch on the ship's propeller was not reacting at all to throttle movements. How stubborn.

I won't get into the electronic interfaces of the system, it would take too long, and I am still not certain I truly understand it all myself. But suffice it to say that ships without workable pitch is bad Juju. I solved and fixed the problem by midnight. Not much time for anything else that day but sleep. And the next day, I had duty. The nightlife would have to wait.

# Life of A Simple Sailor An Autobiography

The following day after duty, I slept until 18:00. I had worked the whole night through. That generally happens as an Engineer in the NAVY while on duty. Once I awoke, I ate and then decided to enjoy the nightlife that was robbed from me the night before.

My shipmates accompanied me to Palma. We found the local dance clubs and bars, picked what appeared to be a quiet establishment and stepped inside. I was in the mood for a little dancing. And maybe even get a tad drunk. After all, it was my duty to uphold the highest traditions of the U.S. sailor.

Though I never fully experienced the 60s in America, and certainly not at an impressionable age, I am fairly certain that what I saw before me was a society literally locked in those years. Bell-bottomed pants and ruffled shirts adorned the locals while they wore headbands and beads. Dancing to sounds of the Bee Gees and Olivia Newton John. Travolta seemed to be everywhere. Platform shoes and large, gaudy medallions were ever so present as well. I had to get out of there.

We stepped into another bar and were greeted by the same crowd. There was an older, Spanish gentleman hogging the dance floor. The movement of his arm pointing up, and then down to the rhythm of "Dance Fever" was causing his toupee to flop up and down. This was almost worth seeing, but my friends vetoed me.

After several more attempts at a decent place to sit, we realized that

Palma needed a few more years under its belt before she became tolerable for us. So, at around midnight, we consoled ourselves by taking a walk down the main street and back to our ship. We were leaving in the morning so a good night's rest would be in order anyway. Our next stop would be Denmark. I was certain we could find something better there.

# Chapter 7

If you fast-forward several weeks, you will find me in Frankenshaiven, Denmark. (Just as a side note, we did stop for a couple of nights in Portsmouth, England via the English Channel. Several of us were selected to participate in a U.N. function sponsored by the Queen Mum. I am going to steer away from this story because I wish to respect her memory. You see, I accidentally touched her butt and, well, it was probably one of the most embarrassing moments of my life.

Frankenshaiven was a small town with no place to park the ship so we anchored out about five miles off the coast. We spent six days there. I did not do much but buy a few gifts and had dinner at a very nice Cantonese restaurant. One particular day however, I think is worth a note.

It was about 20:00 when I decided to take my book to shore, find a nice hole, and read. I picked a very quiet bar that only entertained a few locals. I sat down, ordered a glass of wine and began to read. I nurtured this wine as well as I could, the alcohol there is much more potent than the water here in America. After all, I couldn't possibly embarrass myself without the benefit of my shipmates witnessing it. That would just be rude.

After an hour had passed, the locals became curious. Funny thing is, Americans can be noticed just about anywhere just by sitting quietly alone. The attention started with a small question here and there, but it ended with me at the center of attention. Before I knew it, everyone, including the bartender was buying me drinks. Many drinks. As a matter of fact, I think I drank 10 or 15 beers that night. 10 or 15 more than I usually drink.

They were quite curious about an incident regarding a famous football player that allegedly killed his wife and her lover. I won't mention the trial by name, of course. By this time, it was old news to me and I had the same attitude as most other Americans on the topic. But, it was a hot topic for them. I felt as if I was standing trial for all Americans in regards to the verdict handed to the man. I'm no judge, nor do I know the whole story. I tried to be very careful with all my answers. But what was really important to me was their perception on America as a whole. That trial really hurt us abroad.

Everything else seemed to be quite a blur. I am not proud of this, but I can't give false images of myself to others. It would not be proper. I was quite toasted when I left that bar. But before I did, I made certain that the subject would not be on that trial. I wanted them to think fondly on Americans once I left.

Anyway, it gets worse. Unbeknownst to me, that night was only foreshadowing for the next few nights to come. I don't know how I survived it. But let me try and explain.

During this time of my cruise, we were conducting a Partnership for Peace exercise called "Cooperative Jaguar," which involved the Navies from Finland, Denmark, England, Germany, Swiss, to name a few. To boil it all down, it is nothing more than exercises conducted under way and in port, involving all countries.

We also hosted and attended parties. During this joint operation, many sailors are swapped from ship to ship to promote ideas and lifestyles in good faith. I was one of those that were swapped. The first ship I was sent to was *Her Majesties Ship*, Cardiff from England. This is where my troubles began.

I was sent to HMS Cardiff on a Rigid Hull, Inflatable Boat (RHIB) off the coast of Sweden. Upon boarding, the commanding officer greeted me with a host of his junior officers and assigned one to show me room and board. Once settled in to spend the night, I was taken for a tour of the ship. Though the layout of their ship is much different from American ships, I found that much of the equipment was the same. I guess we all buy from Taiwan. They are pretty cheap, you know.

They took me down to the engineering spaces at my request, for professional reasons. They had diesel engines that were used for propulsion, but the electronic interface was relatively the same as on my ship, which used gas turbine engines for propulsion. Diesels, in my opinion, should be used for backup only. They are too clunky. Know what I mean?

On their control console, I noticed that throttle speed was not making specified command from the pilothouse. Minor, but very annoying. But I had seen this problem before. It really can't be fixed without a complete change-out of wires and components, unless you get lucky and find the elusively loose wire. This problem will be persistent one day, and then it will disappear the next, only to return months later. I pointed out the deficiency to them and they told me that it was a problem that had been recurring off and on for about a month and they had never been able to solve it.

I asked if I could have a multi-meter, schematic diagram of the system and a gopher (someone to play fetch). Once received, I went to work on the problem. Like I said before, you really can't isolate this problem. The wiring system is far too extensive to troubleshoot. Short of replacing each item individually, the best you can do is "hide" the problem. On my ship, there were several strategic places you could hit with a hammer to make the problem disappear for a short time.

But I got lucky this time. While searching for the right place to "hit," I found that the difference in command throttle and actual throttle speed was caused by a sheared lug in a terminal box. I replaced the lug and the problem disappeared, for now, anyway.

They were happy. So was I for now, but at night, my troubles began. You see, on ships from foreign Navies, alcohol is permitted in the dining facilities. The crew took me to the bar and started buying me drinks. I did not want to drink at all, but I also knew I had a responsibility to my ship, the U.S. Navy and the United States in general to be an excellent ambassador. And I was in Rome...

I have learned several techniques to perform this task and one of the most important is to respect custom, and if need be, join in these customs if asked. So I drank. And drank. And drank...and literally forgot most of the evening. I kept telling myself "no more," but they were ever so vigilant in producing a fresh beer when I was half finished with its predecessor. I tried to nurse them, but the Englishmen would have none of it. So, I drank.

The next morning rolls along (along with my head) and my new shipmates were anxious to tell me everything that had transpired. They were not surprised that most of my memory from that evening was more or less lost somewhere. Apparently, after ten beers or so, I started singing and dancing, recruiting others to join in as the feeling suited them. I even went as far as to jump on top of a table with two other Englishman.

They explained that the ship took a roll, and so did I, right off the table and into the arms of several sailors. They told me I arm-wrestled some of them, beating some, until a giant of a man came up for his turn and nearly tore my arm off. I don't arm-wrestle in public, folks.

Then the funniest thing happened, if I remember what I was told correctly, the commanding officer embraced me in a hug and then started to actually wrestle me.

I don't know if I won or lost but before the match came to an end, another sailor picked me up and dropped me unceremoniously by a group of people playing a game of chance. They told me I played, though I could not even begin to tell you what the rules were. After being told this, I checked my wallet to discover fifty bucks missing. Guess I should have learned the rules.

Later that day, my ship picked me up in the RHIB and took me back. My Commanding Officer and the Commanding Officer of HMS Cardiff had a discussion about my performance over the MR Satellite phone that night. I laid low for the next couple of days. Avoiding even my Chief. What would you have done?

Several days later found me in Aarus, Denmark. Aarus is a much better place than Frankenshaiven. The town is not as pretty, but there were more places to go. My shipmates and I spent all our time sightseeing. At night, we spent our time away from the ship in a little tavern called the English Pub. No Travolta there, not even a dance floor. But the music was nice and the ladies were pretty. Couldn't ask for much more.

I met two English officers from *Her Majesties Royal Navy* who were the haughtiest people I have ever met. Every statement they made was an absolute aspersion, and the worst part was they were too arrogant to even realize how insulting they actually were. Again, that ambassador philosophy must come into play. Responsibility can be tiresome at times.

So, I listened to their holier-than-thou attitude for some time, awaiting a slip of the tongue so I could gracefully escape, or slide underneath it with a small comment or two that would set them straight. I thought about the old "We kicked your butt twice" routine, but that didn't seem appropriate at the time, and so overused.

The chance arrived about two hours later. Yes, the conversation lasted that long. The English love to hear themselves speak. Go ahead and ask them, they'll tell you. But I found out that one of the officers was an Englishman and the other was a Scot. (Ever seen the movie *Braveheart*?)

You see, to this day, there is still a small measure of animosity between some Scotland and England fellows. All I had to do was ask the Scot how he felt being a part of the "English" Navy. He stopped his dialog and turned a nice shade of red. I could see the anger in him. It was almost palpable. It took great effort for him to calmly explain his ideals and morals, which of course differed somewhat with the Englishman's. It did not take too long for the two of them to get into a shouting match and eventually, boxing match.

I sat back and relaxed, enjoying the show until the local constable arrived and hauled them away. I wondered to myself if they were from the Cardiff. Wouldn't that be special?

The last day in Aarus, my ship held a party for all the Navies that were with us. I did not participate in this because it required full dress uniform and I really don't like wearing that thing if I can help it. I heard it went well until my ship ran out of beer. Europeans can really put away the beer. Once we ran dry, the party ended with the guests saying it was an insult for running out of alcohol. Go figure. Sometimes, I just can't understand local customs. But I'll share this with you; we spent a good deal of taxpayers' dollars on this stuff just to show our hospitality. I think we should be the insulted ones.

The next morning, we set sail. Let me rephrase, my ship got under way without me. Permit me to take a few steps back here. Two hours prior to getting under way, my Commanding Officer confronted me. For a brief second, I thought of my short tour on the Cardiff, my heart skipped a few beats. My C.O. told me that he had a little chat with Cardiff (Oh no!)…And was pleased with my performance. He asked if I would like to do the same thing on a Finish ship. "Are you kidding?" I replied.

So, I boarded the Finish ship about an hour latter. While the ship was casting off and at "Sea-and-Anchor-Detail," I spent my time in the Chiefs' mess talking to an old salt of a Chief. He told me his history as a sailor in the Northern Blue and what it was like sailing the icy waters (yawn….).

After the navigational detail, several crewmembers stopped by the

Chiefs' mess and took me to the bar. They told me that they had talked to the crewmembers of Cardiff while at the ship's party and Cardiff told them about me. So, they turned around and asked my ship to cough me up for a day or two. For sport, I would imagine. I'm such a pickable fellow.

I couldn't believe how I had gotten myself into this mess. They wanted to get me drunk, this was certain. One thing was definite though, it is 09:30 and I don't want anything to do with alcohol, so screw diplomacy. I used the excuse that, since I am to rendezvous with my ship soon, I was not permitted to partake in spirits of any kind. For some reason, they respected that.

Leaving Denmark signified three great things, warmer weather, the end to drunken stupor and… Lisbon, Portugal. But before we arrived, we had to make a short stop.

# Chapter 8

At one point in my career, I was assigned to work with the United Nations. For the most part, we visited foreign ports and attended social functions. But our real mission was to perform searches on board other ships to ensure they were not doing anything conducive to harm a country allied with the U.N.

I was on the Boarding Team party. Whenever we encountered a ship that was not on official duty (referring to any ship that was not Allied Military), we would board her and take a look around. My specific duty was the Engineer. It was my responsibility to study the structural layout of the ship via use of schematic diagrams, survey the physical layout of the ship and look for any differences there may be.

There are pirates out there, ladies and gentleman. Not the swashbuckling, Jolly Roger flying swordsman you may read about in the days of the conquistadors, but entrepreneurial bad guys looking to make an easy buck by skirting the system. It is very easy to get away with things at sea. There is a lot of open space out there. And the rules only apply if you give a care.

You couldn't imagine some of the things I had found. We have encountered smugglers trying to transport thousands of rubber duckies to another country without paying necessary due diligence. Smugglers shipping any type of drug you can think of. We even have uncovered Plutonium fuel to make nuclear weapons. We had encountered it all.

In most cases, we would just report our findings and let the smugglers go on their merry way. We had bigger fish to fry. No need to concern ourselves with a ship that found a living with transporting sand to far-off lands to place on their rocky beaches. Who cares if they get away with that? What we were truly concerned with was arms dealing, especially the nuclear kind, and drugs.

Humans never cease to amaze me. I have always carried the belief that people are inherently lazy, stupid and afraid. But this particular day added a new item to my thought process as it showed me something about human kind. Something hidden in our closet that I had thought was abolished over a century ago. That day, I added barbarism to the short list.

It was a quiet, sunny day. I was sitting on the main deck by the Gunner's Mate locker, cleaning my Desert Eagle when the Skipper came on the 1-MC telling us to gear up. We had a ship that would not respond to our hails. This could have been anything. Perhaps a stranded ship, a bad guy, even a crew of men that couldn't speak English. Hell, at this point, you never really knew. Our radar showed that the ship was several miles away to starboard. Plenty of time for me to finish cleaning my gun before we were close enough to board.

After we were all suited up in appropriate gear, we took our prospective stations and waited. The other guys were more decked out in weapons than I was. I just carried two pieces. A .22-caliber pistol, and my Desert Eagle. Again, my job was the engineer, nothing more. My duty was more on the study aspect of the mission. Generally I had a sailor or two with machine guns and rifles at my side so I could do this. But carrying a piece certainly was not overkill.

We finally met the ship just over an hour later. They were trying to lose us. Kind of hard considering there isn't a place to hide, and we were much, much faster. But once we were in target range, they were polite enough to stop and allow us to come onboard. Nice to see they remembered their manners just at the right time.

Most ships were grudgingly hospitable in allowing us to board. Due to all the fire power, it would behoove them to do so. But this ship seemed a little different to me. You always knew that they were harboring illegal contraband by the look in their eyes. My first thought was drugs or arms. Both were quite lucrative. Given the fact that this was right after the Gulf War had come to a head, chances were we would encounter the latter.

The ten of us jumped on the RHIB boat and approached the ship. We had a backup of ten more men just behind us in another. I could see sailors running about the ship, tripping and falling over one another. They definitely had something to hide. I wasn't too concerned for myself; these things always went smooth, no matter what they were carrying. But prudence dictated caution. I was always on the lookout for trouble.

Once we arrived, the crewmembers from the other ship dropped a ladder down for us to climb. Wasn't that quite nice of them? As I jumped over the railing, I looked at the crew briefly before I headed out to do my work. I always made it a point to let them see me place my hand on my piece before I did anything else. Perhaps I was just humoring myself, but I wanted the message to come across that I was not afraid to use it. I really wasn't.

As the leader of our mission began dialogue with the Skipper of the ship we were on, my guard and I went straight to Damage Control Central as the other members of our team went to their assigned tasks. They always had blueprints of the ship where they orchestrated Damage Control. It only makes sense, and I had a good feel for ships so I never had any problems locating our destination.

I mapped out the layout of the ship on a piece of paper. This always took time. Generally, I would need to take the ship apart in sections, to ensure I covered everything. Our mission was never over until I had completed this task. I normally started with the lowest levels of the ship, and worked myself upwards until complete. Generally, if they were hiding anything, it would be on the lower decks. My search generally ended there if we found anything.

I mapped out the lower level of the ship, noting all the compartments, berthing spaces, holds and voids. It took time to do this; I had to ensure I had everything perfect. It would not do any good if I missed something as small as a tiny void; the favorite hiding place for all bad guys. Once complete, I was ready to perform my initial investigation. With paper in hand, my guard and I began to leave.

As I was reaching for the arm to the hatch, I felt a tug on my shoulder. The sailor that had escorted us was trying to stall me. Before he could open his mouth, my partner lifted his rifle within inches of the man's face. Quickly, he backed down and started rattling in his own language. I put my hand up and said "We don't speak English. If you don't, this conversation is over."

Without waiting for a reply, I again reached for the handle. "Pardon me," he replied.

His English was quite broken, but I could make out what point he was trying to get across. "Pardon me," he said again. "I was just wanting to know what you are doing and if there is anything we can do to help you."

I replied, "Your English is good, and you are very kind. What we are doing is routine and we won't need your assistance. As a matter of fact, why don't you just stay here? With us, you would only get in our way. I want to get this over with before supper. Besides, the sooner we leave, the happier I'm sure all of you would be." With that said, my guard and I walked out.

He still accompanied us. I just ignored him, but kept a watchful eye. Never could be too careful. And I had my partner with me. I had to use my head here and couldn't keep as good of an eye on him as I should. But that's why I had the guard. He did most of the watching for me. I trusted him with my life.

Once reaching the bowls of the ship, I selected the forward most part of the craft and began my walkthrough. This was a simple process. I would walk the length of the ship and verify that my drawing of the level matched the outlay of the ship. I checked every compartment, scuttle and bulkhead; making mental measurements as needed, to verify the accuracy of the blueprints.

It didn't take long before I came across a portion of the bulkhead that should have had a compartment hatch there. I did not see one. I didn't notice at this point, but later, my partner told me that the other guy with us started to feel a bit uneasy. I looked at our escort and asked him where the hatch was. He told me that there wasn't one here and pointed in the forward direction indicating a hatch about 20 frames ahead.

I went to that hatch and took a look inside. The compartment was not large enough. It should have been twice as big as it was in order to account for the missing space indicated on my diagram. I looked at the escort again and he gave me the "Sorry-can't-understand-your-English-tongue" look. Then he departed in a hurry. I told my guard to be on alert. This man will be back with friends soon…

My partner and I discussed this for a moment and agreed that there should be a room here. So, we walked to the Athwartships passageway, crossed to the other side of the ship, and then walked the length back to where the missing compartment was. No good. There was a room there, but not big enough to accommodate the empty space. We walked back to the side of the ship where there should have been a hatch.

Once there, I called on my C.B. for one of the other fellows on our team to bring a cutting torch down to us. And then we waited. Our tour guide was still gone. This made my partner and me a bit uneasy. I got on the C.B. once more and requested a few more of our men to come down and assist, just in case.

Once the cutting torch came, I instructed the sailor carrying it to cut a whole in the bulkhead. He started his work right away. The smell of burning metal permeated the air. And then, it started.

At this point, things are a bit fuzzy, my mind seems to have blocked out most of this. But what is clear to me is that the escort we once had came back, and he had some partners. They were also carrying guns. I heard the click as one of the muzzles pointed right in my face. I looked down the barrel and saw the face of the man holding it. I felt anger, but stood still. I could hear the cutting torch extinguish. He had a gun on him as well. I could hear one of the other foreigners speaking now.

"All of you just stay calm and no one will get hurt. We have nothing you want and things are going to happen a little differently now, I am afraid." He was a fool.

I looked back at them and said, "What do you think you are going to accomplish here? We have 20 armed men on board here. I just radioed my ship and they are bringing more men. If that is not enough for you to handle, consider the fleet of ships we have encircling you. This is not the proper time for you to attempt negotiation."

After a few seconds of awkward silence, backup finally arrived. Distracted by their approach, the two men and I were able to overcome our assailants. Several shots were fired, but none of my men were hurt.

Stepping over one of the bodies, I walked toward another bad guy and asked him what we were going to find. He would not reply. I asked him again, and he just looked at me. Never saying a word. Didn't matter, we would find out soon enough. I told one of the team members to contact the ship and let them know we had found something. He also requested for our ship to send more people, we would need a larger compliment of arms if we were to take this ship properly.

Then, I heard the clunk of the metal plate hit the steel deck. I turned around and walked over to it. Peering inside, it was completely dark. The smell of death assaulted my nostrils. I looked behind me and asked for a flashlight, one of my buddies responded by handing me his. I turned back around and turned it on.

At first, all I could see were sets of eyes peering back at me. Then, as my eyesight adjusted, things became a bit clearer. I knew what this was. Concerned for my safety, I turned back around one last time to ensure the bad guys were held at bay. They were, and the tension could be felt as if wading through mud. So, I stepped back inside the void.

I counted 15 of them. They were slaves. Men and women taking from there homeland and brought here to be sold somewhere in the Black Market. There were dead members with them as well. They were living in their own foul and waste. The place smelled of death, what a horrible smell. To hide them, the crew members of this ship had welded them into this void, hoping we would not find them. Apparently holding onto the faith that their weakness in hunger would prevent them from causing a scene. Actually, they were right. We never should have found them. And the only air they had was a sounding tube located at the top of this void. At one point, this must have been a fuel or water tank.

I thought I had seen just about everything. It was beyond me to ever think that slavery was still a practice now. I walked back out of the void and approached one of the ship's crewmembers. I looked into his eyes. He was afraid. It was all I could do to keep my hands off of him. I grabbed the C. B. at my waist and radioed my ship, letting them know what we had found. Asking them to send some Corpsmen over as well to help these folks out.

We took custody of the ship, and waited for the Coast Guard to come and take her away. As for the bad guys, I don't think they will be plying their trade any time soon. We would hand them over to the U.N. authorities for proper punishment. And the slaves, we kept them with us for a few days to nurture them back to health. We were still on assignment though, so we couldn't keep them with us for too long. We had another U.S. Naval ship, not part of our task force, come to us and pick them up.

I'm not quite certain what happened to them afterwards. I assume they were taken back to their own country. What I can say is that they will remain free for the rest of their lives. And for that matter, so will everyone else around here, if the Free World has anything to say about it.

# Chapter 9

Upon arrival in Lisbon, our liberty was secured until further notice. We were supposed to be able to leave the ship upon arrival, but certain mitigating circumstances blocked our path. You see, two days prior to entering port, some "Black Beard" on board the ship thought he would try his skullduggery skills on the lock to the aviation storeroom and actually managed to open it. His pilferage came upon some items that he thought he needed more than the Air Department. The items stolen were several different types of grease, which makes me wonder why they stole the items in the first place. Many sailors tend to gravitate toward their lazy side. Don't all people?

On the contrary, I would more likely see them throw grease away to halt their work. Anyway, everyone's liberty was held until the pirate was caught. This did not bode well for the rest of the troops so 12 hours later, when the culprit had yet to be found, the Commanding Officer went ahead and passed liberty call. For the record, the thief was never caught.

My first night in Lisbon was okay; I had no one to go out with so I decided to go alone. I spied a large bridge just to the east of our ship and figured that it was as good as any destination I could find. So I walked.

Along the way, there were local vendors, spread throughout with portable grills, who were cooking and selling chestnuts. I must have stopped half a dozen times. Chestnuts are so expensive in America. Here, they were only pennies. I gorged myself.

After about two hours of walking and not even half way to the bridge (it was farther than I thought) I decided a different mode of travel was in order. I hoped on a trolley, which seemed to be the favored mode of travel for the locals. Once there, a "boardwalk" atmosphere with a harbor of ships greeted me, cradled by small, quaint shops and restaurants. I had not eaten lunch or dinner that day so I endeavored to find the latter.

It was around midnight when I finished dinner, so I searched for that trolley to get home. I found it soon after and awaited for it to come by. While standing there, I was greeted by two young ladies. We sat and talked for a short while. They inquired why I was in Lisbon and I told them about my ship pulling into port. They seemed interested about this so I invited them for a tour the following morning.

So, the next day rolls along and they did not show up during the entire morning. Liberty call went down at noon and I was not about to wait for them, no matter how cute they were. They probably would not show up anyway. I told them morning time, and morning was over. I decided to leave with my shipmates to go to the local flea market. Liberty, if you can imagine, is one of the most precious commodities around. I could not afford to sit idle on the ship awaiting two ladies who would not show up. But luck would have it that while walking off the brow, the two Portuguese showed up. I wasn't at all disappointed in leaving my friends behind.

I got to know them a little during the tour and felt better of myself for it. I can't remember their names, but one was studying to be an actress and even played in some of the local T.V. shows, and the other was studying to become a chemist. Odd combination.

After the tour, they invited me for a tour of Lisbon. I happily agreed. After all, a guide is better than my shipmates at times like this. Especially the female ones. First, they took me to an old castle that was nothing more than a plateau surrounded by a great wall except where the plateau met the sky. There was a restaurant on top with an outside patio at the edge of the cliff that overlooked the city of Lisbon. We sat down and I treated the two ladies to a late lunch.

Afterwards, they took me around the wall, which was littered by vendors of all sorts. While walking, a man stopped me and asked if I was an American. I suppose my English-speaking accent gave me away. I found out that he was an African from Alger and was photographing pictures of the castle for postcards. We talked for some time about places both he and I had been and then he asked me if I would like to be in one of his postcards. So, he took a picture of the city and me as well for one of his wares. I'm in a postcard somewhere. How neat.

After the castle became old, we went to the flea market. Which was more than your average market. It looked more like an outside mall with ancient statues and fountains all over. I met my shipmates there, which was good fortune because my tour guides needed to leave and go to their next class. We shopped for a bit and went back to the ship early.

We set sail and spent the next 45 days under way. This is a bad time for sailors because being so close to one another in everything we do, for so long without a break, is enough to get everyone on each other's nerves. And believe me, it all happened. Arguments all over, fights breaking out at least once a day, tension was thick enough to cut with a knife. But please do not think badly of sailors for this, it just isn't human nature to accept this type of fate without some measure of reprisal.

We went east toward the Adriatic and stopped off the coast of Tunisia where we spent the next two weeks going around in circles. We were doing an exercise called Bright Star and our job was to guard the Marines' landing on the coast of Africa. They were scared of the dark.

Afterwards, we went off the coast of Turkey, Syria and Egypt. Doing the same circles. Well, maybe a little smaller. It was a long 45 days. During all these operations (Bright Star, Morning Star, Vigilance, etc...) we have picked up sailors from each of the afore-mentioned countries.

Once, I stood for one hour straight listening to an Egyptian pilot tell me about his flight time (yawn) and how great he was at it. I did not wish to be rude, so I just listened. Now, Egyptians pilots are probably the best fighter pilots in the world, but this guy was too much. He would definitely have more status marks etched into his jet if he just talked to his enemy, vice shooting at them. Anyway, once all our scheduled operations were complete, we headed toward Italy.

# Chapter 10

We went through the Musenna Straits, which was beautiful, Sicily on the south and Italy north. Each so close I could almost throw a stone either way and hit land. Many fishermen were struggling in their little boats against the wake our ship created. Once through the straits, it was off to La Spetsia, Italy. I'll take you there now.

We arrived in La Spetsia around 09:00. Liberty call went down early, about 15:00. My first day there, I took a train to Pisa to see the bell tower (the leaning one). It was a nice little town with shops everywhere. I wanted to go into the tower but it was under reconstruction, had been for about six years the time I went. But it sits (or leans) next to a beautiful church with a gorgeous lawn, which stretches for what looked like a half mile.

There was also a monastery with a large, stonewall surrounding everything with a huge iron wrought gate at the entrance. I had a nice spaghetti lunch on the sidewalk and spent about two hours afterwards browsing in that little town until it was time to catch the train going to Florence.

Florence is beautiful. Large sidewalks, open squares bigger than football fields. Fountains and statues were everywhere. Old buildings were the motif. There was a church there by the name of Santa Maria Del

Fiore that was so huge, with statues that adorned niches carved in the stone of the façade. Many of the spires and minarets glittered with what appeared to be gold.

I went inside... and did not come out until two hours later. It seemed even larger on the inside, and beautiful. Walking the perimeter of the church, I found it to be in the shape of a cross. Each appendage of the cross, housed a shrine of Mary, Joseph and Jesus, respectively. The length of the bottom shank of the cross was filled with pews except for 50 feet on each side for pedestrians. At the summation point of the cross, stood the altar.

I went to the altar to show my respects to God and, upon my rise from genuflecting; I looked up and lost my breath. Straight above me hovering 500 or more feet high was a concave dome of a painting, which resembled Michelangelo Buonarotti's Vast Frescoes Dome in the Sistine chapel at the Vatican. A complete likeness really; I've seen that one too when I met the Pope. It is gorgeous, but very expensive. Quite the enterprise the Vatican has. God can be quite lucrative at times.

My first thought was that it really came from Michelangelo, but I could not ascertain that. Later, I had tried to ask a priest, but he did not understand the question. It's that language barrier thing.

This church had a basement, a shrine of sorts beneath, that housed the crypts of all the deceased priests that served her. I soon realized that what

I was walking through was not really a basement, but catacombs. You see, many churches of old built in Italy have catacombs they used for burial. Anybody see *Indiana Jones and the Last Crusade*? The catacombs looked similar but you could tell that modern human hands took their toll.

After I toured the church, my buddies and I went to a little café to drink cappuccino and wait for the train to arrive in order to get back to the ship. We had to wait an hour or so, but the atmosphere was so relaxing that I was disappointed when it was time to leave.

The next day, I decided to visit something Roman. So, off we went to the train station to look and see where we could find an old fortress or something. We discovered, in a roundabout way, that there was a Roman lookout post right across the harbor where my ship was moored. No trains had a route that led there, so we had to take a taxi.

There really was not much to look at, nothing awe inspiring. Just a bunch of rocks and an occasional wall half fallen over really. Time takes its toll on everything, rocks notwithstanding. I found a lot of these little archeological disappointments all over Italy.

Without a tour guide, there was not much to glean from this place. The scene was the best part of the whole thing. It stood on a peninsula of sorts and if you stood in the center of the outpost, you could see the ocean beyond. I promised myself to go to Rome if we make a port visit in Naples, Italy. I was certain to find a few Roman things there.

That night, I was on board the ship reading a book when the Chief Engineer confronted me in my berthing space and asked if I would like to attend a banquet on board the Italian ship moored next to us. I know an order when I hear one. I naturally agreed.

The dress was formal so I threw on my gunslingers and attended the party. It wasn't bad actually. There was plenty of food, no beer and no rude Brits. They had a 50-pound wheel of Parmesan cheese, and I think I ate about half of it. I spent most of the three hours there talking with a group of Bulgarian Officers. Pleasant people, but I wouldn't want to be in their NAVY. Upon departure from the party, I snagged another wheel of cheese and smuggled it onboard my ship. Took me a couple days to polish it off.

We left La Spetsia the next morning and headed south around Italy again to make a port visit to Trieste. After two days of duty, I went to Venice. We boarded a train, which took two hours to get there. The memory of Venice will last me a lifetime. I don't think I ever saw a more beautiful city. The lagoon was everywhere. And the walkways, the only way to travel on land, were small and quaint. The shops lining the walkways sat right next to each other as if they were the same building.

Each stood roughly three stories high. Because of all this, it was like walking in a maze. Every once in a while, you would come up against a large plaza, some twice as large as a football field. Rivers were everywhere providing a thoroughfare for gondolas. Small bridges provided thoroughfares for us. I counted 234 footbridges total, but I think there are over 390. We stopped in a small restaurant of my choosing. It was called Jeno's. I thought it was appropriate; mom and dad owned a restaurant back home with the same name.

Jeno's sat at the edge of the Grand Canal which is one of the larger rivers. We sat out on the patio (all the restaurants had patios) and ordered. Two things an American always wants to try in Italy are pizza and spaghetti. I did not know which to choose so I ordered both. I am happy I did this because the servings were quite small for my standards.

After lunch, we decided to get lost in the maze. We window-shopped and talked to local vendors on the street. We made so many turns that I didn't bother to pay attention anymore. We turned one small corner and found ourselves in Piazza San Marco, the largest plaza I have ever seen. Huge ancient buildings that looked to be five or six centuries old surrounded the plaza. I saw the Palazzo Ducale, Saint Mark's Basilica and the church of Santa Maria Dei Frari, which housed the burial tomb of Titan. Undisputed, one of the greatest artists during the Renascence.

Later that night, when walking became weary, we stopped in a small shop called the Quadri Café in San Marco Plaza that had a piano player in front. I ordered an orange juice, which cost, to my amazement, six American dollars. I have never known a more expensive drink in the world except perhaps one time in Japan where I spent the same amount on a coke with less fluid.

I only had one drink there. Afterwards, we decided to head back to the train station even though we had four hours till our last train left. Like I said earlier, we were lost and it took us several hours to reach the station. One of my party members was leading the way, he seemed like he knew where he was going. After about an hour and a half though, I questioned him to see if he knew what he was doing. He told me he was following landmarks that he memorized and "See that green neon cross? I remember that!" He said. So, I left it at that and continued to follow. And follow. And follow, and I saw about ten other green neon crosses since then!

I decided it was time for a new leader. Another one of my team players took charge and started guiding us. And I followed, and followed and followed myself back in San Marc Plaza. Ok, my turn. I decided to let the locals guide us. I asked someone where the train station was and they pointed in a general direction. After a short period of time, I asked another person and they pointed. I continued to do this until we arrived at the train station some 20 minutes later. We hopped on board within 15 minutes to spare and went home.

On the following day, I went to Austria to go skiing in the Alps. We were supposed to go on a tour there which required 30 people minimum participation but we could only get 15 people, so they cancelled the trip.

Well, that was not going to stop my partners and me. Skiing the Alps is a once-in-a-lifetime opportunity. I never gave it any consideration that I have never skied before.

We called several rental car places and found a car that we could rent in short order. We left around noon to go to Austria. This ride will take me four hours so I settled in with a good book and relaxed. Almost all good things have a bad edge. For this trip, the bad edge was Ron. Ron is an imbecile that never grew up and was reared by snakes. I'll mention him several times as I narrate this story.

About one hour into our drive, we crossed the Austrian/Italian border to exchange money and have a snowball fight. A little later, we started rising above sea level and the mountains with their whitecaps came into view. I stopped reading my book to survey the landscape and was not disappointed in the least. The freeway rose above each town and they sat in the bosom of a low valley, cradled at the base of tall reaching mountains. Each house looked like an old fashioned cuckoo clock with balconies on the second level that traveled the entire circumference of the house in which it sat.

They were white with mahogany wood trim. In the center of each town stood the steeple of the local church. Our destination was a town called Kaprun. As luck would have it, our incapability of mastering the Austrian language in one day was the cause of my partners getting me lost.

We found ourselves in Salzburg, which was north of our turnoff to Kaprun. When I discovered their error, we corrected our plan of action in short order and were soon on the backtrack route to Kaprun. I was a little disappointed at this; I was willing to spend a few hours in Salzburg to see if we could find the von Trapp Castle. Unfortunately, my shipmates had no romance in them.

We arrived in Kaprun about one and a half hours later and went in search of our hotel. The hotel we stayed at was called Gasthof Mitteregger, I think. Not certain, I don't speak Austrian. It was 18:00, so skiing for that day was out of the question. They secured at dusk, which happened around 17:00 that time of year. So, after settling in our rooms we went to rent some skies for the next day.

Let's see if I can get an endorsement here. You know that commercial "VISA, it's everywhere you want it to be"? Let me tell you something, I have been to Russia, all the way down to Australia. Everywhere in the Middle East, and have traveled just about everywhere in Europe. Hell, I've even seen the Poles. The only place I haven't been yet, is Central and South America.

Anyway, the point is, I have used my VISA in almost every one of these countries and never had an issue. Never until now, trying to get skis in this little shop located in Kaprun, Austria. It took me an hour to get a cash advance with my VISA at a local bank.

Afterwards, we decided to go to dinner. Once we located a nice restaurant, we sat down for a bite. At dinner, Ron was persistent in asking me for money I did not have. He was such a pest. We made about the same amount, but he kept pestering me so I gave him a few coins just to shut him up. I ignored him the rest of the evening.

After dinner, the gang wanted to go to a bar. I really wanted to go for a walk (and leave Ron behind) so I told them I would meet them there and then left. The sun had disappeared so all lights were lit. It reminded me of a little Christmas town one might find somewhere in the North Pole. It was lovely.

I came upon a small square, which was disarrayed with people in a fiasco so I went to investigate. I saw children dressed like demons and they were actually running around hitting people with sticks and switches. There were many weird customs out there! Spying me, the children gave chase. I did try and avoid the situation as best I could, but it was difficult to get away.

After my walk, or run rather to get away from the sticks, I stopped in the bar and found my companions…and Ron. I settled myself down for a drink with the memory of those kids still on my mind. Curiosity overcame me so I arose and went to the nearest table of people, sat down and introduced myself. Besides, they were cute and I needed an excuse.

It came to be that there is a demon called Krampos who is the nemesis of St. Nicholas. Krampos Day happens on December 5, and everyone dresses up like him to whip and beat each other with sticks. Great custom. The children however start on December 2 to get their licks in prior to the 5th so on the 5th they can hide indoors while the adults take over where the kids left off. Smart idea, if you ask me.

The company I chose to speak to happened to be three nurses from Salzburg. I was enjoying my conversation with these three ladies. We talked about Austria and all the things that can be seen. Their customs and traditions, and we compared them with ours in America.

Well, it came to pass at such time when I was showing them pictures of my family when Ron approached us. He was using me as leverage to gain faith in these women. An old sailor trick, or any man's, really. Apparently, he thought he could, how can I say this politely, have a successful evening with these new found friends of mine.

These nurses were wise to him from the start so Ron was only successful in embarrassing the life out of me. The women eventually had enough of him so said Auf Wiedersehen to me and left. At which point, I left as well. I stiffed Ron with the tab. I thought it was appropriate seeming that he drank about 90% of the bill anyway.

The next day we went skiing. The hotel arranged for transportation to the mountain, which I believed, was called Gletscherbahn, the part of the Alps that resides in Austria. We took a tram that carried us about half a mile up, and then we had to hop some sort of electrical train that inclined at a 45-degree angle, which took us quite a ways up through the mountain. Then we had to get on a gondola that took us the rest of the way up.

I could not imagine what I got myself into; all I saw was unforgiving jagged rock, clusters of trees and a permeating fog that would not lift. It was downright hazardous. I also did not see any skiers. I thought I made a big mistake. But at the top of the mountain, the fog lifted and cradled in the middle of the "circle" of mountains was a "bowl" of sorts where everyone was skiing.

So, decked out in thermal firefighting gear (we had nothing else to keep us warm) we hit the slopes. Now, I have never really skied before so I was starting from scratch. After I mastered standing up on my skis, I felt it was time to try my luck at movement. Bad idea.

After going down the mountain the first time, and not necessarily on both feet, I felt I made a big mistake. I had no business on such a mountain. It was very steep and about one mile long. It took forever to get down. I asked around for the kiddy slopes, but the only answer I received came in the form of laughter.

After many tumbles, I took a small break in the lodge and sat by the fireplace to keep myself warm. Now, there are thousands of people on this mountain so it didn't take me long to reconsider my luck when Ron came up to me and asked for some more money. I just wanted him to leave me alone. I gave him what little I could spare. I was waiting for the hostess to come to me so I could get a cup of tea. I only had a few schillings left because I left my wallet with one of the sailors who had a zippered pouch. I didn't want to lose it.

Ron comes up to me a second time asking again for more money. I told him I only had enough for one cup of tea. Persistently, he asked again and again. He hovered over me like a vulture waiting for me to die. I finally told him to just get away from me. I almost reached my limit there. Sensing this, he skulked away. We never talked much after that. I suppose I burned a bridge there.

We arrived back at the ship early the next morning to get under way. I enjoyed this trip to Europe and there were several more to come. Perhaps I'll share them in another book, but I'm anxious to get to another story.

# Chapter 11

There is a wharf in the Philippines called Navasan Pier. I think I have talked about this one before. Or I will. I haven't put this collection in any order yet. This pier is set on a peninsula, away from all human inhabitants. There are reasons behind this that I will not get into. It wouldn't be appropriate. Suffice it to say that every time we pulled in there, Navasan reserved us a parking space.

Like at most docking times, we needed to refuel the ship. Much the same principle as if you would at the gas station, but on a grander scale. It involves the aid of many people, coordination and time. Roughly eight to ten hours' worth, not to put a finer point on it. This was also a very dangerous evolution. Though I have never seen this happen, dumping fuel over the side, which I must concede is a possibility, would be quite harmful to the ecosystem for months, if not years, to come.

Everyone knew his duty. We would have several personnel designated for sounding tanks, others to manipulate the pump rooms, laboratory assistance for sample testing, messengers. We even placed sailors strategically throughout the outside of the ship to ensure we didn't accidentally spill oil over the side of the ship; this seemed to keep Green Peace at bay.

The connection on board our ship was on the fifth deck, so to set up for this operation; we had to pull the 10-inch hose up from the pier. This was heavy work and required almost everyone's combined effort to get it up there. This sucker was really heavy. And once in place and secured, everyone needed to report to their assigned places. My place, was to remain at the hose and draw samples every 15 minutes or so.

If you're not careful, many foreign countries will try and give you the worst stuff they have. So the standard operation is that I would draw a sample and the messenger would pick it up for delivery to the Oil Laboratory. They would test it and then send the sampled test and results to the Engineering Officer of the Watch (EOOW) for his blessing. He was in charge of the whole evolution.

There is a common circuit on board ships that everyone can plug into with a special phone set to enable you to communicate, no matter where you were on the ship. We called it the "Sound Powered Phone." A clunky device that included a headpiece for hearing and a small diaphragm-operated mouthpiece that's mounted on a small breastplate. While refueling, everyone involved wore this device.

This particular day was pleasant, not too hot. It was still morning though. Later on in the day, it would get very hot. There was some shelter to cast shadows about, but I was also concerned with the humidity. It can get quite nasty out there, even when it is cool. I knew if everything went smoothly, I should only be in the worst of the heat for a couple hours. But something always seems to go wrong. I never considered the possibility for what was about to unfold.

Once the pumps started, I drew my first sample by pouring the fuel with the aid of the test connection provided, into the one-pint glass sample bottle. I had a whole box of them at my disposal. Giving it to the messenger for delivery, I reported to the EOOW that it was on its way and then settled myself down in the shade. I wouldn't have to take another sample for the next 15 minutes.

Looking out into the water, my mind started to wonder, the voices over the circuit seemed to drown out to almost nothing. I enjoyed the morning time, no matter where I was, as long as I could look out into the ocean. Watch the sun rise. See the birds, an occasional dolphin, playing in the background. The cool breeze coming off the waters with a hint of salt in the air seems to always lull me in the most comforting way. It is quite soothing, to say the least.

Right before the next sample, I noticed a coconut on the deck. Not certain on how it got there. I picked it up and threw it in the ocean. Unlike what you see in the grocery store, coconuts picked off the tree have a very large, and very hard husk surrounding the little brown ball. Watching it bob once or twice, I turned back around to draw my next sample. There was another coconut lying on the deck on the other side of the platform I was on.

After drawing my sample and making my report, I looked around for a reason why they had come to my deck. The palm trees were distant, so they just didn't fall there by chance. My first thought was that someone had picked them, and then carried their trove on board; dropping a few along the way. But the thought that also occurred to me was that I probably would have noticed them before. I'm such a sleuth.

Then, suddenly, another coconut came rolling to a stop next to my feet. I looked up and saw a monkey sitting on the railing on the deck right above me. Did the coconut come from him? Wouldn't surprise me. I've seen stranger things in this world. Then, shortly after the first monkey was spotted, a second one came to rest on the same railing with a coconut in his hands.

It was time for my next sample. Turning my back to the monkeys, I grabbed another bottle and drew my next sample. While wiping the oil off the bottle, I was assaulted from behind with a solid hit in my lower back. I turned around and saw the coconut lying by my feet. I looked up and saw the pair of monkeys jumping up and down, making a bit of a raucous. They seemed quite pleased with the direct hit. I made a comment or two to my little instigators, picked up the nut and threw it in the ocean to join its partner.

A short time later, several other monkeys had arrived, all carrying their own coconut. I was getting a tad concerned here. Watching them carefully, I distanced myself from the monkeys and took the empty sample bottles with me. They were quite expensive, no need to take any chances. But they just stood there, watching me and holding their respective coconuts.

When it was time for the next sample, I took another bottle out and started to pour. At that moment, two more coconuts came flying my way. These monkeys were pretty good shots, and coconuts hurt. One hit me in the thigh, and the other in the shoulder. I was getting a bit angry now. Looking up, I saw monkeys with empty arms leaving, only to be replaced by those carrying more coconuts. "This can't be happening," I thought to myself.

After the sample was taken, I spoke on the sound-powered phone headset, "EOOW, I have a bit of a problem here. You see, there are several monkeys up here using me for target practice with coconuts. I think it would behoove us all to send a few men up here to deal with the situation before something serious happens. Perhaps a few trashcan lids in hand would be in order?"

Immediate laughter followed. Everyone on the circuit heard this and couldn't stop laughing. They thought I was joking, but used it as sport to make merciless jabs at me. It was sort of funny, but not at the time. The EOOW didn't believe me, even when the messenger had verified my story with his own eyes. The folks on the circuit thought he and I were playing a practical joke.

So, for the next hour, I'm taking my samples while dodging these coconuts. And ever so vigilant was I in requesting aid. This was turning into a rescue operation, to say the least. I really needed some help. I couldn't just abandon my post, which would mean big trouble. So I continued to request help, only to receive more bantering from the sailors.

I was blasted on every portion of my body with these coconuts. These monkeys were having a great time, it seemed. And their accuracy was getting better with every throw. And at one point, they hit my sample bottle. This means war.

I gave the broken sample bottle to the messenger and told him to deliver THIS sample straight to the EOOW. A few moments later, the EOOW speaks on the circuit, "Mr. Powell, I can appreciate a good joke like anyone else, but this is getting a little old. And to try and support this crazy scheme of yours by purposely destroying one of my sample bottles places you in serious risk of Captain's Mast! I want you to stop this charade RIGHT NOW!"

I was completely at a loss for words. But for a moment, only. I tried to calmly explain to the EOOW that this indeed was happening, and I really needed some help. Everyone else on the line, of course knowing sailors, was providing their two cents' worth when the timing was right. Some of it was constructive, some rather insulting, but all in good, unclean sailor fun, nonetheless.

Finally, the EOOW had had just about enough. I must admit though, it did take much longer to reach his limit than I had originally thought. I was waiting for this moment.

"Mr. Powell, this is a serious operation and you are jeopardizing it with your little antics. You are dangerously close to finding yourself in deep sh#t. I am heading up there right now with your replacement. You do not move a muscle!"

As I stood there, realizing how precariously my career teetered on a wire, I looked up at my troublesome friends and gave them a little speech, "Look guys, you got me into this mess, and you need to get me out of it. There is a really angry fellow about to burst out of this door. He is so angry with me right now, that he is liable to do just about anything to make me pay for what all of YOU have done. When he comes out that door, I want to see how good your aim really is. If not, my cooks know a recipe or two that they have been dying to try out!"

The EOOW came storming out of the scuttle. Looking right at me, he didn't notice the sudden volley of coconuts. About 10 came dashing toward both of us. As he approached me with death in his eyes, "WHAM", right in his temple.

Nursing my own bruise from the most recent assault to my chest, I looked down at the EOOW, lying on the deck. He was a bit dysfunctional at the moment, but he was conscious. I then looked up at the monkeys. They were jumping up and down on the rail again; happy with their new target, and the bull's-eye they had scored.

I helped the EOOW up and looked right in his eyes. It was not necessary to say a word to him. After a moment's pause, the EOOW took my headset and spoke to the troops, "Gentleman, this is the EOOW. I want three men up here on the 05 level with a trashcan lid in both hands. Do this now..." And then he walked away, never looking back, rubbing the side of his head.

I don't know if it was vindication, or the clumsy efforts made by my benefactors attempting to protect me with trashcan lids. But for the rest of the operation, I couldn't keep the smile off my face.

# Chapter 12

This story is a little delicate for me. It took some time to come to terms with what happened. As a matter of fact, I believe now, that I started writing this set of stories to help me come to terms with little issues like this one. In every sailor's life, comes one point in their career where something so profound or traumatic assaults them, that it changes their outlook on life forever. This one is mine.

There is a set of maritime laws; rules to follow when you are out to sea, that all NATO-sanctioned countries follow. Some had been established as recently as yesterday; some are as old as lore can remember them. But they were all established for the good and welfare of any person troubled at sea.

We were following a path southeast, making a slow travel to Korea. I had just dried off in the shower after an 18-hour workday. I would have the next six hours off. A goodly amount of time for any sailor underway. I can remember many days where four was all I was afforded. And speaking of four: that was the longest stint of time in days I had ever worked without any break. Six hours was a blessing indeed.

It was about midnight when I heard the call over the 1-MC for all available hands to report on the main deck. Refugees had been spotted off the port bow. According to Maritime Law, it was our obligatory duty to pick up these helpless souls. After hearing the message, I donned a pair of pants and my shoes before rushing up there. The excitement masked my weariness.

It was a calm ocean that night. The moon was out in full swing, casting light everywhere it could penetrate. Regardless of this, we still had our port lights on. The wind was barely present, but it was enough to provide a faint rustle that picked up my short-cut hair, tossing it from side to side. And it was warm too: about 70 degrees, normal for this time of year out here.

I was one of the first men on the scene. Spotting where all the activity was, I joined my shipments just forward of center port. Three men were there, lowering a Jacob's ladder into the water. Grabbing a rung to help transfer the ladder over the side, I looked down for the first time. What I saw, I will never forget.

It was a small boat, about 20 feet in length. Made out of wood, I could see several spots where the pitch could not hold the water. There was no motor, no oars, nothing seemed to be used to propel the small vessel. They must have been floating out here for days. Weeks even, who knew. It was just blind luck that we bumped into them. I don't even think we could have spotted them with any of the technology we had on board. And the U.S. NAVY is ranked about third in the world, when it comes to technology.

## Life of A Simple Sailor An Autobiography

My eyes first met a young lady, holding a baby in her arms. The child could have been no more than three years old. She had the look of resignation in her eyes. The thought that we were there seemed to never penetrate those eyes. She clutched her child close to her breast. At first, I thought the child was dead, or asleep at the least. But a slight movement of the head showed me that I was, thankfully, wrong.

Giving a pause, I looked at the boat in its entirety. There were about 15 people crammed in there. 15 that were alive. Several of them, I noticed did not make it this far. When refugees flee their country, it is assumed that they will not make it through to safety. But they feel the great risk is worth it, just to leave their country. Hoping that on an off chance, a shift of the wind, a measurement of fate, would bring them to safety.

I was the smallest and strongest for my size. I was chosen to climb down the ladder and help these people up. At this point in their journey, it is known how weak and feeble they are. They probably have not eaten in days. They are malnourished, dehydrated and on the brink of death. They would need help climbing the ladder. That was my job.

Once I descended to the bottom of the ladder, my heart took a step back. Lying on the deck of the small boat closest to me was the rank of death. Not only that, but the looks of the corpse told me that it was not days sense they had eaten, but perhaps hours. It took all my efforts not to faint from the sight. I don't know what was worse, the thought of

117

cannibalism, or the smell that came from it. A tear came from deep inside my soul as I grabbed the corpse and threw it into the ocean. The refugees watched my movements, but that was the only reaction they would permit me.

One by one, I hauled these people up the ladder. By this time, more of my shipmates had arrived to assist. Some of them were hanging above me on the ladder to take over when my reach could not extend any higher. These poor people had over 20 feet of vertical ladder to climb.

I grabbed the boat at one point to bring it at a better angle. The refugees were so fatigued, they could hardly move. As I reached out, I had noticed for the first time that sharks came by to give us a visit. Some of them were in frenzy, making a meal of what I had discarded in the ocean earlier. There were more like the one I threw overboard, but I knew in my heart that dumping anyone else would do more harm than good. These sharks were actually reaching their heads clear out of the water to take a swipe at me, or the person I was hauling onto the ladder. I had to be more careful.

Once I repositioned the boat, I was able to get more people out. Just a few more to go. The lady I had spied earlier with the child was moving closer to me. One more person I grabbed. And then another. And one more.

She and her little girl were the only ones left on the boat. The only ones alive, that is. She set the child down and reached for me. I would have preferred to have the girl first, but she was already in my arm. I hauled her up to the next fellow on top of me. I went back down for the little girl.

Suddenly, the ship took an unexpected roll. We pitched a little to starboard, and then sank deeper to port, just enough to put my legs in the water up to my knees. I was frightened about the sharks. Forgetting the girl, I moved myself upward, climbed a little higher on the ladder to keep myself safe. I didn't move a muscle until the ship steadied herself.

I climbed back down and reached for the girl. She was just inches away. She couldn't move. She just laid her head on the side of the boat, resting it there; looking at me with what little hope her troubled life would give her. I couldn't reach her; I needed to go down just a bit further. About the same spot I was at before. After getting there, I reached out once again and took hold of part of the shirt that clothed her shoulder, and the ship moved. Again, I was not comfortable, so I took my hand back to grab the ladder, readjust my hold with the other, and then turned back around.

It happened so slowly. The memory is even slower in my thoughts whenever I think about it. The nightmares it has given me since are fading now, but the vision still remains. I will never forget that night, the night we stumbled across those poor refugees. I will never forget the look the lady had given me when I first set eyes upon her. I will never forget that little girl, and the hope she dared to give me. And I'll never forget how my fear and selfishness interfered with my duty. How, once I felt comfortable, to turn around only to see that last flash of hope in that little girl's eyes. Right before it was replaced with shock, as that hungry shark lifted itself out of the water, grabbed hold of her tiny, little head and took her beneath to its home.

I instantly started to cry. I hated myself, I hated my shipmates, I hated the NAVY. I don't know how long I held onto that moment, but the screams of my shipmates brought me to, somehow. I just wanted to jump into the water and join the little girl that I failed. She deserved at least that much. And then the torch came. Landing square into the center of the small boat, it didn't take long for it to ignite the wooden craft. Again my shipmates were calling for me. It was time to go.

As I looked up, ready to climb, a shark had somehow grabbed the ladder. Its mouth was caught on a rung. It had attempted my foot that was in the water, but luck moved the ship at the right time. Anger filled me again. Hate that I never knew was there. I grabbed that shark by the gills and lifted it out of the water. Not certain what to do. Maybe I could just hold the demon there until it drowned. But I did not move. I stood there, one hand holding the ladder, the other holding the shark. A death grip. I sneered in its depthless eye.

I suppose they knew I was not going to move. I felt the tug first, and then my shark and I started to ascend up the side of the ship. This angered me as well. I could not drown the shark if they hauled me up, they would throw it back in. I was infuriated. I began smashing this shark against the side of the ship. One pound after the other, after the other. I was not going to allow this shark to live once I let it out of my grasp. I felt it needed to die. I hated this shark. And I hated anyone that would prevent me from killing it.

As I reached the main deck, and before my shipmates could do anything, I lifted the bloody shark over my shoulder and threw it on the main deck. Most everyone that was there, spread out. I leaped over the arms that reached out to help me over. I went to the Boatswains mate closest to me and grabbed his marlinspike out the holster he carried around his waist. I did not notice if anyone had tried to stop me.

I turned one last time on the shark. Approaching its flailing body, I commenced stabbing it in the side several times. The skin was thick; my penetrations hardly made a dent, but it made me feel better. Much better. That little girl died because of me. But so will this shark.

I felt the arms come over me in a wave. Five or so of my shipmates had to hold me down. It took me moments to calm myself. Afterwards, I started to cry again. I don't know the shipmate that held me, but I cried like a baby in his arms. I really needed that. It is what brought me back. I loved that shipmate for being there for me. Whoever he was.

The next morning I awoke and carried out the plan of the day. No one spoke of the shark incident, we had more things to worry about. Like taking care of the survivors. Feeding them, clothing them. Nursing them back to health. But to this day, I don't know what happened to that shark after I was done with it. Nor do I even know the name of that sailor that rescued me from certain insanity. Now, it is just a bad dream.

# Afterthoughts

I enjoyed my 13 years in the NAVY. I don't regret a single day. Even the bad ones hold their own unique quality; they are what make me the person I am today. But all in all, it was a wonderful experience from which I have learned lessons in life that can't be taught by a scholar standing behind a podium.

I could have had a very nice retirement if only I stayed for another seven years, but I left the NAVY to spend more time with my two children. My father once told me that once you start having kids, your life stops and theirs begins. That was the soul focus on my decision to get out. A "no-brainer" really. It took me a very short weekend to make that obligation to my kids.

I have so many more stories I would love to share, and perhaps I'll write another book to do just that. It is 04:00 in the morning and I'm sitting in the dark here in my little apartment. Feet propped up on my computer stand, writing these last few sentences. I already have several stories of some of the things that happened, ready to go on paper. But it's time to get ready for work.

As I look over the dark room I am in, I can hear the hum of traffic pass in the street nearby. I am not ready to let this book go, but I think it is time. As I glance down at my propped feet, I find myself staring fondly at that little black O-ring around my ankle. I'm thinking I will start that new book tonight.

Printed in the United States
211798BV00001B/96/A

9 780972 070584